Rosie's Gift

Published under licence by Brown Dog Books and
The Self-Publishing Partnership, 7 Green Park Station, Bath BA1 1JB

www.selfpublishingpartnership.co.uk

ISBN printed book: 978-1-83952-134-8
ISBN e-book: 978-1-83952-135-5

Cover design by Kevin Rylands
Internal design by Andrew Easton

Printed and bound in the UK

This book is printed on FSC certified paper

Rosie's Gift

BEVERLEY JOUGHIN-ROBSON

PART ONE

CHAPTER 1

Looking through the photograph album, Marjorie paused at the small picture of her younger sister. She hadn't seen her for years; almost twenty years in fact. They grew up during the war. She was born in 1933; her sibling was born three years later. The small child in the tatty black and white image was holding a man's hand – her father. He had been very strict, probably a result of his years in the Army (he fought somewhere in India) and his own stern upbringing. She knew her father loved his family, but he was very distant and awkward around them. It was her mother who gently guided the two sisters through their early years. She could still imagine her mother's soft hands wrapped around her own tiny fingers and remembered her wide, warm smile. Everyone told her what a very loving and caring person she was, when they stood around the coffin on that notable November day in 1941.

Turning the page, she fingered the aging photographs, too few to give a clear idea of her childhood, but enough to spark the sporadic memorable images she could muster in these quiet, contemplative moments. The photograph she stroked lovingly now, showed her young mother at the kitchen window, looking out, probably watching her children or enjoying the view of her well-cared-for garden. She was happy to have the two bundles of mischief in the kitchen with her, baking cakes and preparing vegetables. A smaller photograph of her parents showed a happy couple, obviously in love, holding hands, sitting on a wall, in front of an expanse of beach; the sea stretching out, a pale grey backdrop, insignificant against the warm, loving smiles of these two lovers. She had never known the young people in this photograph; they were alien to the two people she remembered as her parents. Their father was an electrician by trade. He was very precise in both his work and his expectations of his family. He was very handsome, Marjorie decided. Another picture affirmed this thought, his bronze, spectacled image in khaki shirt and shorts suggesting a brave youth.

Marjorie turned another page to the few pictures she still had of her and her sister. A few scattered moments, two at the farm, one at Trafalgar Square, and a couple of family occasions with older relations she did not recognise. A tall man looked out at her from the back of the small group. She knew him as an uncle who had died at sea, but that was all.

There were few great events during her childhood. Life and pleasures were simple family routines – except for the war of course. Living in Tottenham, they were in the midst of some of the harshest bombing. Marjorie remembered the school being shut for a brief period in the cold winter month of January and part of February 1940. It soon reopened and the 'normality' of life returned, apart from the gas mask she had to carry round, the practice air raids in the iron shelters on one side of the playground, and a few empty desks where once school friends sat before they moved away, were bombed out or were victims of the attacks. The memories of school were the same as before: trundling through the multiplication tables, writing stories, learning spellings and drawing lots of pictures. And her sister had been a part of that world. Now she suddenly longed to see Eileen again, after all these years.

Marjorie was about three or four when she felt an imminent change in the house. An anxiety hummed nervously during the daily chores. Although a war was threatening, for a young toddler there was just an unsettling and troublesome flurry of concern, interspersed with the usual playing in the garden, walking to the shops, and busy activities which engaged her mother as she looked after the new baby. She had watched her little sister with pride and interest. The photograph of her holding this small child awkwardly for the camera was now nestled in her hand. After all this time she had made contact. The war had torn them apart at such a young age and now she was coming back into her life. It was a shock. A wonderful, daunting shock.

Marjorie remembered how she had watched the dark, heavy, black curtains, pulled purposefully onto rails, at the windows, blocking out the light. A heaviness absorbed the airy front room and her bedroom became sinister and threatening. Several of the local children had been labelled up like parcels and sent off on a train to another part of the country where it would 'be safe'. One little boy, Charlie, was bundled off to a place called Norfolk.

"We ain't got no choice. Dick's joined up and me mam's takin' us in since we lost part of the back room. She ain't got no room for us all. We'll bring 'im 'ome again if it don't work out," she explained to my mum over the fence one afternoon.

Packed up with the items on the proposed list: one vest, one pair of pants, one pair of trousers, two pairs of socks, handkerchiefs and a jumper, plus a few added items, some shorts, a coat and good, strong shoes, he joined the queue at the station.

It wasn't until the bombs started dropping nearer to home that Marjorie's parents had sent her and Eileen off to find sanctuary.

There was an air-raid shelter at the bottom of the garden, built following the pamphlet of government instructions. Eileen was only a baby and Marjorie was only about four, as they watched their father and a helpful neighbour dig the large, deep hole. It took nearly a week to complete the shelter. There was a heavy piece of metal with bumps, corrugated iron it was called. It was bent over the hole to make the roof for the cell they would hide in on various occasions. Mud concealed the makeshift bedsit, their underground home where they would wait and wait and wait. Sometimes the endless, tedious waiting would bore the youngsters into sleep. Other times, Marjorie remembered playing cards with her mother while Eileen played with her dolls or drew pictures – scribbles really. Marjorie felt a haunting fear as the incessant exploding bombs vibrated and dully echoed like thunder above them, sometimes dismantling small pieces of gravel and earth, dislodged by the tremors. But mostly she just remembered being bored! The adults seemed to have a greater sense of fear.

On a couple of nights, the children were carried outside as the sirens went off, to the air-raid shelter, in their nighties! One particular night when they were running over the damp, scraggly grass, weeds and earth, the sky lit up with sporadic explosions and beams of light, like fireworks, as they scuttled into the shelter. This was the worst time, Marjorie reflected, glancing once more at the last few photographs before putting the weathered album back in its drawer. She didn't remember the tension or the anticipation which silenced them as they snuggled under the bunks' covers, but she clearly remembered the image of her mum nervously making tea, and still heard in her mind, the tremendous crash and resounding thud that stilled them that night.

The house had lifted and moved about a foot with

the impact of the bomb, so close you could feel the force shooting through the ground like an underground train. It had killed the goldfish. Danger was accepted, unlike the lack of food, although they were lucky enough to have the blackcurrants and black and red berries, when they were in season and growing wildly at the bottom of the garden, just behind the shelter. Of course there was a glut of milk and the joy of eggs and chicken when they were evacuated to the farm, but that was no consolation when they had been taken from their home.

Marjorie was about seven and Eileen four when they ventured south. They joined the group of worried faces, smaller children clinging to older siblings; all with their brown tags, small but heavy cases and mothers holding onto or hugging their children, trying not to cry. Mrs Davidson seemed to be quite happy to lose her brood. There were lots of children in her house. Marjorie's memory failed her, but she imagined her mother would be very tearful; her father was probably offering words of encouragement in his very efficient way. Marjorie was to look after her little sister and 'set a good example', like her father had told her to. He had stood firm and resolute as they climbed up the steps, following the other children. The metal bar was cold and hard and they felt a similar coldness seeping through their coats, even though the air was neither damp nor devoid of the sun's heat. Perhaps it was the tears that were welling. Marjorie knew neither of her parents really wanted to send their children away, but death was knocking at the doors of their street and the neighbouring streets.

The train journey was actually quite exciting.

"Where are you going?" a tall girl asked the pasty-faced girl next to her... She was sitting opposite the sisters and seemed keen to talk and make friends, but Marjorie was happy to sit quietly and watch and squeeze Eileen's hand with a motherly, comforting gesture.

"Don't know. To a nice lady and her husband."

"Rubbish. It ain't nice. It's a horrible old farm." The sour-faced boy of about six turned his bottom lip up with an indignant force, making his heartfelt annoyance permeate the carriage.

"The country is full of animals, cows and sheep and ducks and things from my picture book," gabbled a more hopeful companion. The speculative chatter continued, though most heads bobbed quietly to the rhythm of the train as it trundled along its tracks, away from London, from the safety of home and its dangerous bombs, to the dangers of an unknown place and the safety of the country. Eileen held tight to Marjorie's hand. She was now her responsibility and Marjorie felt the burden, feeling panicky as the bricks of Tottenham were replaced by the fields of rural England. They seemed to be leaving civilisation behind.

The vast expanse of green and gingerbread-coloured fields, were awash with speckled yellow and white blooms of flowers that Marjorie recognised from the jumble of grasses in her own back garden. The tall wisps of strange grasses, alien to them, bristled as the speeding train swept past. She had seen some animals in the zoo, in London, but the grey and white balls, spotting the hills and the fewer, closer, nonchalant cows, huddled by the hedgerows, cowering under the bushes, absorbed her thoughts for a while and eased the pain she felt.

"How far is it?" Eileen's voice interrupted the silence. Eileen's loosened grip gained strength as her own anxieties returned.

"I don't know. Quite a long way, I think," she guessed. The two sisters sat quietly for most of the journey, until Eileen closed her eyes, lulled into her own world of dreams, while Marjorie drifted off into a fitful sleep, thinking about her mother at the station and then in the kitchen, mixed with the new sights from outside.

When they arrived, the brusque, dangly woman, with the rather narrow eyes and contradictory, warm smile, met them at the station and ushered them into a random circle on the platform. Eager faces, excited though cautious, were caught uneasily in the woman's gaze, like rabbits in a spotlight, as they followed her instructions. Eileen and Marjorie followed a plumper lady, Mrs Thompson, to a tired bus, which would deliver them to their new home. The Smiths greeted the two tired tots at the end of a gravel and mud path, which would lead to their farm. They stood in front of the awkward collection of planks of wood, forced together, resembling a gate.

There was a strange, pungent smell that they did not recognise and unfamiliar noises. There were no vehicles or banging and shouting of doors and squeals and cries emanating from children, instead there were small noises like whistles; timid and twittering reverberations from above and squawking announcing the arrival of an insistent bird.

"Marjorie, look!" Eileen jumped back, pulling her arm, her hand still tightly encased in her big sister's hand. A large fowl with scruffy feathers waddled up to them suspiciously, followed by others and Eileen began to cry.

"Don't you worry, they warn 'ert you, thems ducks," the lady laughed. "Lots of thers 'ere. And chickens, an cows, an the like," she continued.

They looked at her apprehensively.

"Call me Antie Joan," she welcomed. "Now follow me anyways and I'll show you yer little room, then you can help me in the ketchin."

She was showing us kindness but there was a stiffness about her movements and awkwardness from not having children of her own. The loss they felt for their parents back in London weighed profoundly.

The small room, which was to be theirs, had just the one small iron bed but it was neatly dressed with a pretty blanket of different-coloured holey squares.

"You like the blanket, I see. Crocheted it meself, I did," she beamed.

"Anyways, put your cases down, there's lots to do in the kitchen and Alf will want 'is tea when he gets back from the fields."

Alf, or Mr Smith as they called him, said little but tended to grunt and bark orders at everyone, including his wife. He was a gruff, scruffy, broad man who bossed Auntie Joan about unnecessarily, and seemed to be devoid of interest in the children. He spoke to his animals with a greater tenderness, although Auntie Joan seemed to love this workhorse. She kept the children busy, helping to make bread and jams. Marjorie became a great help, too, when she got the hang of milking the cow and feeding the chickens, collecting eggs and cleaning. Sweeping and cleaning were her usual tasks. Eileen was far too young to be much help and was often left to her own amusement, chasing the cat and ducks around and attempting to sweep or try her hand at the simpler chores. They got on with their lives, working hard to help out now that the young man they had hired had left to join up. There was an awkward kindness and when their mother wrote asking for their return now that the bombing had become less frequent, they couldn't wait.

But only Marjorie would return. The telegram arrived while Marjorie was eagerly folding her sister's small jumper that her mother had knitted, packing their few belongings into a case. The bomb had ripped up most of their street.

There was nothing left of some of the houses and theirs had suffered badly at the back, where the kitchen was. Her mother had died instantly. Her father was on leave, in the back parlour. His arm and leg had been caught by flying debris and he would be coming home from the hospital in a couple of days. The Smiths wanted to keep Eileen, and her father would not be able to cope with such a small child. Marjorie would be needed to help in the house and look after her father.

The first week she busied herself around the house, cooking, cleaning and enjoying keeping house and helping her father. She tried not to let his anger and sharp tongue affect her love for him. She tried not to fuss, which made him worse. A few weeks turned to months and her own frustration and tiredness made her more irritable, though she hid her feelings well, remaining upbeat and cheerful for both their sakes.

Marjorie waited patiently for her sister to return, writing letters that she hoped Auntie Joan would read to Eileen. Her father recovered physically but he hardly spoke and seemed to shrivel up, sitting staring at the mantelpiece and the picture of her mother. One day, as she returned home from school, having picked up the small loaf the shopkeeper had kindly kept under the counter for her, he was gone. It was nearly a week later when they found his body. Marjorie never knew what exactly had happened but she heard people talking about 'the shame of it!' The neighbours took her in, helping themselves to whatever they might need from the house, which was most of their belongings, and she never saw or heard from her sister again. The Smiths had moved away.

Marjorie wiped a tear away, before she realised she had been crying. Then Jim tapped on the door.

"Are you okay?" Jim asked gently. Marjorie looked up at her husband.

"Yes, just looking at the old photographs...of Eileen. And remembering." Jim had been wonderful. Marrying him had been the best thing she ever did. Her own little family had brought her such joy and helped heal the loss of her sister and parents. Little Rosie had been born first and then they had Sam and now they were all going to her sister's wedding in Scotland.

CHAPTER 2

Jim had not been Marjorie's first boyfriend. She was engaged to Ron. She had met Ron when she was seventeen, at a dance. He had a genuine smile and affectionate manner. She would walk to the end of the road to meet him so that Mrs Beeton, Winnie, never saw his motorbike. Winnie had been a wonderful substitute mother but with four children of her own, she was quite strict and 'ran a tight shop', as she was often heard saying. She liked Ron but did not approve of the bike.

In those days, Marjorie was like most teenagers: she left school and studied to be a secretary. She learnt shorthand and how to type at Pitman's College, preparing for office work. It was expected that she would meet a nice young man, God willing, get engaged, get married and have children. She would not have to work then, she would have a man to do that. Her job, like all married women, would be to cook, clean and look after her home and family. She envisaged her future with Ron, a semi-detached home and children, working as a secretary until then and organising meals and the home, while Ron worked hard in the local garage. But, like most plans, life gets in the way and while on holiday with a friend, she met Jim and fell in love. The attraction was deep and fascinating. His dark brown eyes and easy confidence had her hooked. She broke off the engagement with Ron and broke his heart. But youth can be easily influenced and her life was to take a new path.

The first night she stayed at Jim's she slept in the little spare bed, in the front room. The light filtered from underneath the heavy grey and pink patterned curtains. Although it was a rather drab morning, she felt a lightness not affected by the weather. His mother, a tall, willowy lady with merry, mild, blue-green eyes, came in and woke her with a cup of tea. Her smile radiated kindness. She ran the home with a firmness and control but a sensitive gentleness that remained with her throughout her life, passing her caring amiability onto her grandchildren. She seemed to know her son would marry Marjorie, and only weeks after their wedding she gave her one of those all-knowing smiles and said, "You know Stanley says you're going to have a little girl."

Jim's dad, Stanley, was a quiet man. He sat smoking a roll-up in the back room by the fire that was dispersing the chill as a welcoming gift. He was small but had the presence of a man in charge of his domicile. He was known to be right about most things and Marjorie's heart skipped with delight at the thought of having a daughter. "Rosie": the name seemed to speak to her like a strange premonition. She had no idea why she had suddenly conjured up such an unusual name but she liked it and placed the thought neatly at the back of her mind, to consider in a few months' time.

On that first visit to Jim's home, Marjorie wore a fluffy, pale pink mohair cardigan, with little pearl buttons, her favourite, reflecting the softness and love that she was feeling. It was wonderful to be enveloped in happiness emanating from the warmth of a family. This just added to the attraction she had for Jim. They married in February 1955. It was snowing. The winter flakes, like confetti, caught in the wind, following her and her father-in-law as they walked confidently towards the church. Fervent onlookers waved. Her bouquet of lily of the valley brightened the winter scene. For Marjorie, her wedding was as expected, the best day of her life, except of course for the birth of her children.

When Rosie was born Marjorie wept, not just with the pleasure of holding such a beautiful child, but for the sister she had lost. Rosie was a gift from God, she was convinced.

CHAPTER 3

The small three-year-old moved quietly among the bushes, picking at the flowers aimlessly. Her parents, aunt and uncle chatted openly and enthusiastically about the forthcoming wedding of her mother's sister, Eileen, in Scotland. Rosie was unaware of her importance in the discussion, her dark locks hanging loosely over her delicate shoulders and the little white collar of her new yellow dress, bright against the olive-green leaves of the bush which absorbed her, as she watched the ladybird crawl intensely along the branch, fluttering its tiny wings cautiously.

Just a few months earlier, Marjorie had caught her daughter turning the pages of her treasured photograph album, rather heavy-handedly, and had rushed over to grab the book from her, when she stopped abruptly at the small child's excited cry, "Ile-leen!" She said it only once, but Marjorie was sure she had pointed at the picture of her sister and said, "Eileen." She immediately doubted it. Rosie was only two years old and she was learning lots of new words. She was copying. She must have said something that sounded like it. She was learning to talk and say all sorts of things. But just two weeks later her father-in-law had taken his granddaughter for a trip to Scotland 'on business', and returned with the news that he had been trying to find her sister there. Eileen had been living with the same Auntie Joan but her husband had died tragically: "a farming accident," he was told. That's why they had moved away, up to Scotland, to live with Joan's sister, running a bed and breakfast business. Marjorie could not help thinking her tiny daughter, Rosie, had something to do with these revelations, despite the fact that this was ridiculous and impossible. After that, she wrote regularly. It had been a wonderful coincidence that she had found her sister when she did. She was getting married. Such an important moment in her life and Marjorie would be there to see it. She was quite nauseous about the whole thing, but her excitement at seeing Eileen... and Aunt Joan far outweighed any nagging doubts.

They were standing in Jim's brother's garden. His wife Penny was stunningly dressed in her pink pencil dress and delicate pink shoes with kitten heels.

"I must say, I am quite curious and a little jealous of this sister of yours. I am happy being an only child of course, but getting back together after all this time, it's such a happy ending to your sad story," Penny enthused. Marjorie was less enthusiastic. It had been such a long time. She was apprehensive. Would they even like each other? The fact she had asked Marjorie if Rosie could be a bridesmaid convinced her that she was probably still the sweet little girl she left behind – only older of course. She returned her attention to Penny who was returning from the kitchen with a lemonade for her and a small glass of wine for herself. Marjorie preferred lemonade. She and Jim rarely drank. She quite liked a port and lemon or a snowball at Christmas. Jim liked a beer occasionally, too, and was at the moment tasting a new batch of bitter that his brother John had brewed.

"Rosie will make a beautiful bridesmaid, she's so excited," her mother chirped, glancing round to take in the pretty picture of her daughter. Suddenly their eyes met. An expression of concern caught the mother off guard.

"He's going to fall in," the child warned – not with words spoken aloud but with a mindful presence that seemed almost telepathic. The mother scoured instantly the corner of the garden for the baby chair where she had left her eight-month-old son. It was empty and her beautiful boy was at the edge of the murky-green pond about to topple forward. Instinct is swift, and she grabbed at the slimy cotton vest and hauled him from the clutches of the weeds and sticky tentacles of the plants that wanted to hold his chubby limbs fast. She pulled him up. The spluttering infant cried out in alarm but was safely cradled now, in its parent's arms.

"Oh my God! Is he alright?" Cries of panic and relief were mingled with the concerned adults' comforting arms.

"I didn't see him – I shouldn't have left him sitting so

close…" Words of remorse and guilt tumbled uncontrollably from both parents; the mother now shaking with the realisation of "What if?" In all the commotion, Rosie began to cry and drew their attention from the now gentle sobs of her tiny brother.

"Oh Rosie. Thank you!"

Passing the brother to her husband, Marjorie rushed over and gathered up the yellow bundle and hugged Rosie generously.

"Thank you…my little princess."

It was a private moment and in the general hysteria and drama, the rest of the adult party did not seem to think anything of this rather strange outburst, other than it was a mother's abandoned concern for both her children that had engulfed her senses. And as the drama played out, until all were settled, engrossed in gratefulness, the family continued with their thankful babble and no more was said. In fact, I am sure the mother had forgotten the surreal moment of a child's dreamlike warning and only remembers the traumatic incident as one of a lucky escape.

The life Marjorie had once envisaged with Ron was now being fully played out with her husband Jim and their two delightful children. Eileen's wedding had been a wonderful success, and the last letter Marjorie received from her announced the news that she was expecting their first child in the new year. She was going to be an auntie.

She read the letter again before placing it in the drawer with the others. Their weekend in Scotland had gone so fast. It was a small affair with just the two aunts, Eileen, David her husband, his younger sister and mother and a few friends. There was a warm welcome – but they were strangers. The reception was in the small hall attached to the little local church. It had been decorated with chains of silver paper bells and cream and pink roses. Eileen looked beautiful in a long, white satin dress, embossed with delicate roses to match. Rosie wore a pink dress with a large, cream satin bow, holding her posy tightly, sensing the importance of the occasion.

After the service and the buffet, other friends arrived and the small gathering of people danced and drank, enjoying Eileen and David's special day. Jim was comfortable with the new members of his family and chatted happily with David's father and friends; Marjorie, however, was rather overwhelmed. She didn't like to talk about the past to Eileen on her wedding day. Most of what they needed to say had been penned in their letters anyway. Auntie Joan sat quietly next to her for much of the evening, enjoying the spectacle. They had little to say to each other but there was a pleasant security between them, established all those years ago on the farm.

Marjorie watched her son, Sam, toddling around with the other two small children and talked idly with Joan and the other mothers who cooed over her pretty little daughter.

Rosie had enjoyed all the attention but stayed with her mother most of the evening as if sensing her struggle to socialise with people she did not know. Perhaps her mother was trying too hard. Auntie Joan was also enamoured with the little girl. Rosie knew the old woman was desperate to pick her up and place her on her lap, but her legs were stiff and painful with arthritis. She knew she wanted to tell her stories from the past about when her Aunt Eileen was a little girl. That is what she had been thinking about most of the evening. Rosie kindly helped by edging towards her, looking up with one of her captivating smiles and asking, "What was Auntie Eileen like when she was little?"

The opportunity was seized and the old lady began to indulge in the delightful stories of the past, which she treasured so dearly. Marjorie looked across the hall, fixed on Eileen dancing with David, and smiled. She listened sporadically to Joan's tales and realised that too much time had passed between them. They were sisters, tied together by a bond secured when they were small children, but they were so different now. They would never be close again, and despite watching Eileen from just a few yards away, she was aware of the huge gulf between them. After the wedding, with promises that they would meet up again soon, they said goodbye and hugged, but in their hearts, they knew the distance and their differences would keep them apart much longer than they had hoped.

They both wrote once a week for almost a year, then the

time between letters lengthened until they were writing every couple of months, always sending birthday and anniversary cards and an extra longer letter and parcel with gifts at Christmas. Eileen was careful not to send news again of any forthcoming pregnancies. The letter to Margaret explaining her miscarriage had been unbearable to write. She would wait until much nearer her time, to avoid any disappointment and heartbreak. Next time. But there had been one further miscarriage and then nothing, and Marjorie's chatty letters about her own children had become difficult to read. When Marjorie wrote about their move, Eileen sensed a sadness in her sister that she had not felt since they were very young children, on a train, travelling to the country, leaving behind their home and the mother they would never see again. She sat at the table and started to write, hesitating for a moment, and then, placing the pen back down she sobbed, emotionally drained by years of guilt and grief; she was not sure whether she was crying for herself or for the children she might never have.

When David arrived home from work that evening he had news, news that would mean another move, news that would bring another dramatic change to her life, news that would need to be broken carefully to the sister she had finally caught up with after all these years, only to be parted again and this time maybe forever. They were moving to Australia.

She picked up the letter on the hall table, already

stamped and ready to be posted, and opened it. Picking up the pen, she added a PS at the bottom: "I would like to visit you as soon as you are settled in your new home."

CHAPTER 4

Rosie at six years old was moving away from the home and comfort she had known since birth. A nauseous, nagging weight defined today – today she was starting a new primary school, in a small village, a few miles from where she had grown up; it was closer to her father's place of work. Only last week she had arrived with her mother to say goodbye to her closest special friend, Sharon. It was a Thursday, and on Friday Rosie's family would climb into their Morris Minor and travel the 22 miles up the road, away from the security of the life she had always known.

The two girls sat on the doorstep of the porch, with their Penny Brite dolls still dressed in the same pink dresses the dolls had arrived in; Sharon's was minus a shoe, lost somewhere in a pile of toys. They bent their dolls' legs to sit them down side by side and then Sharon crossed her little fingers around Rosie's smaller, whiter fingers and began to cry.

"I don't want you to go away."

"I know," Rosie replied, "but it will be okay and you will have lots of new friends. Jessica is a nice little girl."

"Who's Jessica?" Sharon looked quizzically at her soulmate.

"She lives in a sunny place by the seaside, but she is going to sit next to you in class, when I've gone. Be kind to her, she's lonely. I'm going to miss you and be sad for a while..." Rosie trailed off.

They sat for a while holding hands and smiling at each other.

"Thankyou for coming to my parties. I liked your blue skirt with the butterflies." Sharon leant over and gave her friend a kiss and then jumped up and skipped off to find the kitchen and a drink.

Rosie sat for a minute looking longingly at the garden where they had played so many times. The swing hung, still now, waiting for someone to wake it up. The roses looked full and heavy – their petals full of perfume waiting to be gathered and left in jam jars of water to ferment. The playhouse's door, winked open invitingly, although now seemingly abandoned.

Last August, when Rosie and Sharon were splashing about in the blue, hard-plastic swimming pool with a dolphin embossed on the bottom, she'd picked up the yellow teacup floating gently and filled it with water.

"Here's a cup of tea for you."

"No, thank you, a bird might have pooped in it or there might be wee wee in the water... Mummy said so." Rosie screwed her face up with the unpleasant thought. Rosie knew that wasn't the case; the water was fine, but she went and got her an ice pop from the freezer instead. The bright blue, raspberry-flavoured icicle was handed over with all the friendship she could muster. When Sharon dropped it in the water accidentally, she decided the ice would clean any germs, so it didn't matter. Sitting on the towels, drying in the sun, the two friends giggled and chatted, playing house and cooking up make-believe menus, until they were delivered to their own beds and families.

Sharon was an only child and liked playing with Rosie; her friend knew things, showed her how to have fun and be happy. But she never warmed to Rosie's little brother. He was either crying or sleeping in the large Silver Cross pram parked in front of the kitchen window, and when he started toddling, he kept breaking her toys, stamping on the delicate arms of her dolls and poking at the eyes until they became detached, giving them an eerie deformity. He pulled her hair when no one was looking; her mummy called him a "naughty little boy"; she thought he was bad and mean but then she didn't know any other little boys and perhaps that's what all boys were like. But she loved Rosie. Her dark brown hair and dark, smiling eyes were hypnotic, and she always seemed to make things alright.

A few weeks earlier she'd lost her little green purse with the beads sewn on in flower-like patterns; she liked the way they felt and sparkled like miniature Christmas baubles. Rosie told her not to worry, they'd find it. After hunting for a few minutes, Rosie held it up in delight, waving it enthusiastically.

"Here it is!" It had been dropped and found its way, awkwardly, between a few stones, behind the apple tree. If she hadn't seen it glinting there as it struggled beneath a pile of mud to be saved, it would have been buried, never to be found.

Children move on very quickly, however, and a few months after Rosie had left Sharon behind, Sharon had a new friend, Jessica, who had moved up from Cornwall. The teacher had told her to sit in the empty chair, the one that had belonged to a pretty, dark-haired girl, almost forgotten by the lively six-year-old who'd been so distraught when her friend had left, except for the occasional dream and insistent memory. For Marjorie, the wrench away from her friends and the home she had built was sudden and unwelcome. She felt caught in a whirlwind, led by her husband's decisions and as dependent on him as her children were on her. At times of insecurity, she questioned her life briefly, but all seemed less daunting now that she had found her sister. She missed her friends and the home she had loved but she was part of a new life now. The last letter she received from Eileen was quite unexpected in its emotional content. As soon as she had settled into the new home, Eileen was coming to stay.

It was a good-sized semi-detached house, nestled in a neat cul-de-sac, centrally placed, looking down the road leading up to the eighteen similar properties housing lively families. A few polite bungalows cosily tucked away in an end corner peeped through established trees, homes to the more elderly neighbours. As it was early July, the sun smiled on the arriving party with a warm welcome. The dark red, newly painted door gave the impression of a cared-for home as the family ventured inside.

Rosie's mother had only seen it once before. Her husband had bought it because of its locality and its modernity in contrast to the older, colder, Victorian two-bedroomed house they'd left. She was apprehensive and obviously missing her established life – her friends, her neighbours, the home she had built over the last seven years – like a nesting bird. Rosie understood and felt a similar apprehension, but her concern for her mother was instinctive as she held tightly to her hand. The gesture gave the comfort it intended, and her mother was distracted enough to look down, linking them with a warming smile.

Rosie's brother, Sam, tumbled up to the front doorstep, lunged through the open door and dived into his new abode; full of unleashed energy, he eagerly investigated the sparse rooms. He was unaware of his family's pensive mood as he stopped at one of the many boxes, grappling at the cardboard.

"Toys! Sam wants his toys…"

"Not now, love, let me make a nice cup of tea first and get you some squash. We'll have the sandwiches and cake

I've brought." She engaged her motherly tone, lightening the atmosphere. The thought of the food replaced that of the toys and Sam shuffled purposefully into the kitchen, full of units and various cupboards to appeal to his curiosity. Mrs Birch scooped up the playful boy and sat him firmly on one of the chairs that had been abandoned in the kitchen by the removal men.

Rosie watched her family thoughtfully, particularly her younger brother, and smiled. This would be a good place to grow up in and would have lots of happy times, although a dampening cloud loomed over her vision of some tears – inevitable of course. Suddenly she sensed a further sadness for her lively brother, and gentle tears were triggered simultaneously.

"Don't cry, sweetheart." Her mother gathered her up with her usual comforting technique and pulled a lock of hair from her wet cheek.

"You'll love it here, I know," probably convincing herself much more than consoling her daughter.

"It's okay, Mummy. I know you are feeling lonely but you said Auntie Eileen is coming to stay and this is a nice house and the lady across the road... She likes you very much."

Rosie's mother put her down warily. There had been several occasions, as she observed her daughter growing up, that had unnerved her. She seemed to know or guess, or say things uncannily correctly; coincidences she knew...

but so many? Usually dismissed, her words today were more poignant. They were warm and heartfelt as usual, but she responded this time.

"How do you know, Rosie?"

Feeling uncomfortable, Rosie thought quickly...

"Oh, I saw her at her window and she just looked like she could be your friend. I could feel it and I just know everything will be fine," she replied with an assuring air.

Marjorie Birch smiled. She was just a very positive, kind and thoughtful child. What could anyone want more from their offspring?

Rosie now had a room of her own. Having shared a room with her brother for three years, the adventure of having her own pink palace was nothing more than magical. At the moment, however, the wallpaper, splattered with farmyard animals, a few trees and shed-like barns, was scrawled across, with unsightly biro, coloured pencils and pens. Probably a mischievous little boy like Sam... "No," she reflected... twins, a little boy like Sam and a little blue-eyed girl with a bright, sparkling smile. Her thoughts returned to her brother suddenly; he was always making a mess or destroying anything that might stand in his way of frantic play. It was not with an unkind meanness, she was sure, but a wild lust for adventure, exploration and uncapped excitement. Looking over at the wallpaper, her father reflected her thoughts and commented:

"It looks a bit of a mess, doesn't it? But I will decorate your room first, starting this afternoon," smiled her father. Rosie could already see the beautiful cream wallpaper with dainty pastel flowers growing in rhythmical patterns across the walls and a new pink carpet instead of the shabby grey-green one, discoloured and worn. The ceiling and windows would be shiny, white and bright, replacing the blackened, grimy sills, which had been cleaned with the purpose of a quick sale but neglected over the years.

"Thank you, Daddy," she answered with a genuine smile of pleasure, although she knew there would be plenty of other jobs to do at the request of her mother, before the mission of decorating her room was addressed.

"Jim! The curtain rail is coming off the wall!" Marjorie shouted, breaking their rare shared moment. He winked warmly and left Rosie contemplating the image in her mind.

It was two weeks later when Eileen arrived. Jim met her at the station. As he drove her back to the house, she was able to talk about Australia and prepare him, hoping for his support, when she came to break the news to her sister. Jim felt immediate concern for his wife. She had been very emotional lately and, although he had been sympathetic to her moods over the move, he had been rather irritated. He felt rather ashamed now and would be more supportive, he decided. As he drove into the drive, Marjorie came rushing out, drying her hands on a tea towel. There was a real warmth this time between them. She seemed much happier now her sister had arrived to stay for a few days. It was a special moment that suddenly made them both blub and hug in the most affectionate embrace they had ever had.

"Oh Marjorie, I've missed you so much."

"I missed you, too. Let's enjoy our few days together and make the most of our time now." She grinned. Jim took his two lively children to the park, allowing the sisters some time to talk together. Marjorie gave Eileen a brief tour around the kitchen, lounge and dining room, stopping quietly at the dresser where a glass coloured bowl forced its attention.

"Was that Mum's? I remember it."

"Yes." The short reply lingered. "It's all I have left," she added protectively. "A neighbour acquired it after the bombing and gave it back to me when I got married." They instinctively held hands again before Marjorie bustled her sister upstairs, to settle her into Rosie's room. Sam would share his room with Rosie temporarily, an arrangement he was excited about. Rosie was simply accepting of the situation, a little peeved at giving up her newfound independence; a room of her own.

"I'm sorry we haven't decorated it yet, but the bed's comfy and it's lovely and light in here."

"It's fine, Marjorie. I'm only here a few days and it's you I have come to see. I hope Rosie doesn't mind too much." The two women made their way back downstairs to the kitchen and a cup of tea. It was then she told Marjorie her news. She noticed the sadness in her eyes and the sudden tight grip of the cup she was holding. To suddenly be ripped apart again seemed so unfair. But Marjorie smiled, easing the rigidity of the moment. She was aware of her own sudden pain but also of Eileen's obvious excitement about moving to Australia. Eileen showed her some pictures and gabbled enthusiastically.

"It's a new job for David and he hates what he is doing now, and I love the thought of being away from the countryside at last and living in a busy town."

She paused suddenly to reflect on her reservations.

"I'm going to miss my friends...and you."

"It's very exciting for you and a new start." She was genuinely pleased for Eileen and hoped the change might bring a baby, too, without voicing these thoughts which lay heavy on her sister's mind.

"We don't see too much of each other now. We can continue to write and hopefully one day we can come and see you in Australia," she added with an enthusiasm she did not feel. Australia – the other side of the world. The chances of her visiting she knew were almost as great as landing on the moon!

Lightening the mood, the two sisters sat chatting casually about their own lives and friends, occasionally holding hands when the conversation drifted to talk about lost memories and a few childhood moments they shared.

Eileen listened to the tales Margaret remembered of her parents and their early years, although for her it was like listening to someone else's stories. The earliest memory Eileen had was of the two of them and a train journey.

When Jim returned with the children and fish and chips, they ate hungrily, laughing at Sam's chatter about his exploits in the park and smiling at Rosie's renditions of the same events. Marjorie shared Eileen's news with her family as Jim rested his arm thoughtfully over her shoulder. She nestled into him, absorbing the reassuring comfort as Eileen's pictures were passed around. The children were fascinated by this country, the other side of the world.

"What a lovely family you have," Eileen mused. Rosie looked wistfully at her aunt. She was sure her aunt would have a boy and a girl, just like her mum…when they were in Australia, but she sensed the sensitivity of such thoughts and said nothing despite the longing to tell her about the family she would have and how happy she would be. Rosie, even at this very young age, was quite aware of how upsetting such an outburst would be for them all, but also aware of the powerful premonition settling comfortably in her vision of the future.

It was a short visit, but a time spent that would remain fondly in their memories always. When Eileen climbed back on the train, Marjorie's family were all there to wave goodbye. Marjorie and Eileen hugged again, this time with a strength of love that would keep them close however many miles there were between them.

"Don't worry, Auntie. I'll look after Mummy!" Rosie shouted. "And so will I," Jim added. He held Marjorie's hand unexpectedly and squeezed it tight to reassure her. After the goodbyes, Jim helped Eileen up the steps with her bags and into the carriage. She settled back in the seat, gazing out of the window, wishing she had her sister's hand to hold onto, tight and reassuring, once more.

CHAPTER 5

Rosie's father was rather transient in her early life. "Daddy's working." To a small child this meant maybe a brief moment and a kiss in the morning, and maybe an occasional recollection of a strong hug and gentle kiss when curled up in bed, lingering towards sleep. Weekends of course were different. Mummies worked in the house: "housework". They cleaned and washed and ironed and went shopping and got cross. Of course, Rosie and Sam had their own jobs, tidying their bedrooms, taking out the dishes and helping to wash or dry up, putting their toys away and using the carpet sweeper on the carpets after they'd made a mess. But these chores were more designed to keep them busy and out of trouble, rather than real, productive cleaning and Sam only got in the way or made things worse most of the time.

Like most fathers with their daughters, Rosie was his little girl, his princess and that meant strong carries and cuddles – when he had time – and a large, firm hand enveloping Rosie's small one; it meant a deep, solid voice, secure and commanding, helping her ride her bike, his firm grip on her back as he held her steady, watching her little legs moving round and round wildly, waiting for the moment she'd take off alone. He was enamoured with her calm and confident nature. She never worried like the other children about the "What ifs?": it was as though she knew she could do things and she had a satisfied confidence almost as if she could visualise her successes before they'd even happened. He was very proud. That's why it was so difficult to be as warm and understanding with his son. Sam was more negative, frustrated and naughty. Of course he blamed himself. He probably didn't give him enough attention or not enough discipline, or perhaps managed punishments poorly. In fact he was rarely punished because a smack only made him worse and if sent to his room, he'd just smash things up. No, he was a very different child and the sooner he grew up and learnt to behave, the better!

While Mum was busy with her work, Rosie would watch her daddy mowing the lawn, big hands pushing the machine up and down, long, straight lines forming, as if by magic. Rosie had to sit on the step, 'out of the way' for this, but when it was time to wash the car, she was allowed to use the sponge, dunking it in a bucket of soapy bubbles and rubbing it up and down the shiny metal car. Getting wet didn't matter because there would be some nice, warm clothes on the airier indoors later.

"Be careful of Mummy's flowers, Daddy," she called as her father threw down the hose, just missing the geraniums coming into bloom. Her grandmother had given them to her mum just last week and they were treasured; some colour brightening up the rather plain view of lawn and concrete path. Rosie's father had dug a piece over for Marjorie to plant some flowers, but money was short and just two small shrubs adorned the muddy patch.

"Well spotted, Rosie," called her father. Rosie had learnt how to give advice and warn without predicting. Over the last couple of years, she had noticed a few of her playmates shy away and adults gave her querulous looks when she spoke of things she felt. Rosie was not psychic or anything crazy like that but she had uncomfortable urges or reactions, like warnings, as well as positive vibes and feelings of encouragement, that she would voice to others. She had learnt to make such intentions less obvious, with suggestions or advice that would secure the safety of, or prevent an unpleasant outcome for, the person involved. Her advice and ideas were offered reservedly and with a nonchalant manner. It was rare that anyone noticed such anomalies, forging a familiar pattern within the family.

Marjorie had noticed the possible catastrophe which was to befall her precious flowers from the window, and smiled at her husband's quick and thoughtful manoeuvre. Standing neat and beautiful was the cherry blossom tree that had made her feel more welcome on her arrival. It was still in blossom but its pretty pink and delicate petals were gently forming a carpet around its base, on the lawn. Such beauty brightened the deeper, darker moods that seemed to swamp her these days. Her family were everything to her: her husband, her children, her in-laws. She missed her own mother terribly. She was only ten when she was left looking after her father at home, most of the time; her education suffered and her own life was put on hold. When her father died it was almost a relief. He was drunk most of the time and she endured his wrath regularly. When she met Jim, she was eager to leave her own family behind her and make a life of her own. She loved his parents and they seemed to adore her. She looked warmly at her children now and felt the heat of a mother's love, forgetting her misgivings and "counting her blessings". Rosie and her brother had missed the last week of the school summer term because of the move. She hoped with the six weeks stretching out before them they would all settle into their new home.

Over the next few years, Rosie positively welcomed the change, indulging herself in village life enthusiastically. She was a member of the school choir and she went to the youth club on a Friday in the village hall. She made friends easily, selecting those children who she knew were kind and thoughtful, and she was an enthusiastic member of the local Brownie pack. Sam raced around his new environment causing havoc but enjoying the sense of freedom; he had his own room to create chaos in and his big sister to look . out for him.

On the Wednesday after her aunt's visit, Rosie met her new neighbour Mrs Blakey. She was tall and elegant in appearance, clutching her daughter's hand while she spoke to her mother across the fence. Sarah was a year younger, with a quiet disposition but a bright smile and compelling green eyes. They would be good friends despite the age gap.

"Marjorie, why don't you come round for tea with your two? The children can play in the garden until Jim and Patrick get home from work. We can all eat together."

"That would be lovely. Thank you. As long as you don't mind Sam, he can be a bit of a handful."

"Oh don't you worry about him... he's just a boy. He reminds me of my sister's middle child, full of mischief but just as cute." She smiled warmly at Rosie's mother. That made two friends now; Mrs Blakey, Brenda and Pat Davidson, the lady from across the road. Marjorie felt a warm pleasure for the community that was beginning to grow around them.

As Rosie selected her toys to take next door, she glanced at the tea set. She hadn't played with that for a long time. The memory of the paddling pool and of Sharon swept silently but quite vividly into view. Pausing for a quiet moment, she gathered them up. They were going to tea and her cooker and tea set seemed the right choice.

It was a pleasant afternoon, recognisably warm but clouds came and went, signifying the threat of a slight shower later on. Sam brought a ball, but he'd set his sights on the pedal car he'd eyed in next door's garden. The child's golf set and their black and white cat, Socks, also warranted his attention. Rosie didn't foresee any harm, just a lot of running about and excited shouts. The cat would disappear as soon as they arrived, but Sarah would be a problem. All she seemed to do was whine and cry. She didn't really know how to play or share, and needed time to come to terms with her new neighbours, Rosie thought generously.

As soon as the door opened, Rosie gently passed her bag of toys to Sarah.

"Let's go and play with my tea set and your play kitchen," she suggested, smiling reassuringly and holding her hand softly.

"What a good idea. Sarah had a new kitchen set for her birthday. Only yesterday she was complaining she hadn't got anyone to play with," Brenda informed her mother. Sarah turned gingerly towards her playroom and Rosie followed. Sam was ushered out into the garden, to his delight, where he explored and chatted enthusiastically to the cat, which was keeping its distance under a garden chair. The mothers sat with a cup of tea, getting to know each other and discussing the occupants of the little cul-de-sac and other characters in the small village which was becoming more of a home every day.

"You know, your Rosie is a real poppet. Sarah is a bit of a loner and yet she seems to have taken to Rosie. It's good to see her sharing her new toy, too… most unlike her," Brenda offered thoughtfully.

"She does have a way with people. She'll make a good teacher or nurse one day," Marjorie reflected.

Suddenly Rosie leapt up, spilling the plastic plate of biscuits she was about to hand to Sarah and rushed into the kitchen.

"Sam's not safe..." she cried. The unexpected drama caused her little playmate to burst into tears and her mother to rush out into the garden, just in time to find Sam, grappling with some shears.

"Sam, put them down!"

"I'm cutting the lawn like Daddy," he protested. She smacked his hand. "Naughty boy! They're sharp and dangerous." Rosie's mother was shaking, annoyed at her own stupidity of just leaving him to play, upset by the events which had dispersed such a pleasant afternoon.

"Thank you, Rosie." Words she was aware she had said on many occasions. "Sometimes I think you're a better mother than me. You are always watching him," she said resignedly. Rosie just smiled and turned to her new companion. She took her hand and gently wiped a tear away, leading her back into the playroom. Brenda had watched and said nothing until now: everything had happened so fast.

"I'm so sorry. I thought they were in the shed." And her eyes followed the two girls back into the house. "What an amazing child you have." The story was retold over tea, when their husbands returned. Marjorie and Jim, reacting to the events with a sense of normality, were a little surprised by the admiring parents but unquestionably proud of their daughter.

Rosie was beginning to get a reputation for her quiet demeanour and loving manner. She was almost too good to be true but Sam helped balance the books. His boisterousness was more evident because of Rosie's gentleness and seemingly 'perfect' behaviour. He suggested a reality that most other parents encountered on a daily basis. And Jim and Marjorie were happy with their contrasting family bundle.

The summer continued with days of colouring, Lego building and puzzles when it rained; when the sun shone, picnics, making tents and running around in the garden. The park was also a regular haunt for Rosie, Sam and the other children of the village, providing an outlet for their playful energy and an abandoned freedom, with a few parental rules and restrictions to keep them happy and safe. Sam would try to escape through well-placed gates and fences; he would try to jump off or climb precarious objects and run wildly and dangerously onto busy paths and the occasional road. Rosie would be there to warn, catch or advise him in the right direction. But she knew the time would come when she could not save him. He would be grown up by then and only he could define his future.

CHAPTER 6

On a gloomy November evening, when Rosie was eight years old, her father drove up the drive in the dark, contemplating his late entrance to the family home. They would have eaten tea by now and he felt weary. He hadn't expected work to take over his life like this and he felt oddly estranged from the family, from Marjorie, at that moment. He paused before going in, wiping some ice off the car and covering it with the blanket, so that it would start in the morning. It was about 7.30 and Rosie was getting ready for bed. She fingered the numbing frost at the corner of the bedroom window, waiting for her mother to return after settling her brother in his room. When she finally pushed open the bedroom door, Rosie felt her sadness. For a while now she had been perceptive of her mother's growing unhappiness, but was unsure why this feeling bothered her so much. In her usual direct and confident manner, she asked:

"Why are you sad, Mummy?"

"I'm just tired," she sighed heavily. She had been thinking of her sister lately, happily settled now with a small daughter of her own. Her own marriage had somehow become a chore. Jim was always so busy and so much less attentive to her these days.

"Tired of us?"

"Oh no, sweetheart, just the housework and having no money and your father works so late most evenings…" She suddenly looked embarrassed.

"It's okay, Mummy. In my magazine, *Bunty*, one of the children's mummies goes back to college and she becomes a teacher." Rosie embellished the story a little to help.

"What about her children?" She spoke, interest piercing the tone of her voice.

"Oh, the little girl goes to school and her smaller daughter is picked up after nursery by a lady who lives near her – her friend," Rosie informed her creatively.

That night she heard her parents speaking, raised voices mixed with quieter moments and finally her father's resounding voice: "No!"

This very definite response secured the present situation and a resigned contentment followed, allowing Christmas to come and go with the usual hustle, bustle, excitement and happiness.

There was an insecure quietness about the house leading into the new year. Rosie was compelled to take charge. At just eight years old, she was confident and determined enough; the quiet and delicate nature, she assumed, fooled most.

One afternoon after school, at the beginning of February,

Rosie after watching some television, and after reading some of her *Secret Seven* book, darted into the kitchen as her father's car drew up. The kettle had already been boiled and the mug and tea bag were waiting ready for his cup of tea, the most important ingredient of the recipe she had planned. The door burst open with the force needed to gain entrance – a DIY job that was still waiting its turn. She greeted her daddy enthusiastically.

"Hello, Daddy, I'm making you a cup of tea. Mummy is having a chat next door, she'll be home soon," she gabbled. Rather amused, Jim sat on the wooden stall and put his briefcase down, removing his coat, which Rosie gathered up eagerly and went to hang on the banister. "Now what's this about?" her father conjectured.

"Mummy–"

Jim looked annoyed and tried to avoid his irritation. "Has she said anything to you?"

"Oh no, Daddy, but she's sad and I've got an idea to make her happy."

"What makes you think she is unhappy?" He was slightly amused as well as frustrated by the interference of his eight-year-old daughter.

"I just know." She paused before setting her plan in motion and handed him his cup of tea.

"Why don't you go on holiday for a few days – grandmother would love to have us, I'm sure, and it's half-term next week or you could go when we break up for

Easter. It's just a thought." She finished with an engaging and endearing pout and then added, "It doesn't matter."

Her voice was soft, like a wounded animal, and then she hugged her father warmly.

"I love you, Daddy." She sat quietly beside him, picking up her book, not pushing the matter any further.

"We'll see," was his final response to the unexpected situation and he sipped his tea.

For Rosie's plan to work she needed to make sure her mother was not reluctant to leave her precious children. She looked down at her brother's small hand, immersed in her warm grip. Sam was nearly six now and attended her school. She walked him the few hundred yards from their house to the red-brick building of the village school, past the red-brick wall that encased the beautiful rose garden of Mrs Christie, an old lady who was hardly ever seen but who opened her garden to the villagers every other year during the Rose Festival. The church opened its doors, too, and the local vicarage invited visitors in, the choir busily volunteering to serve a choice of cakes and light lunches. They were dressed in the customary Elizabethan costumes, elegantly restyled to accommodate the children each year. Mandy bustled forward, followed by her friend Lorraine, to serve Mr Cooper, a favoured customer, who would indulge them with his war stories as they took his order.

"You forgot the teaspoon," he winked, and they rushed

off to scramble through the cutlery tray, now emptied of small spoons. Mrs Smith was slow to wash up and the eager girls took over washing and drying, before returning to wait on tables in a flurry of enthusiastic helpfulness. Rosie particularly warmed to this occasion when the scent of hundreds of vibrant petals adorned the church aisles and windows. Her own name was often referred to on these occasions by the locals, with bright welcoming and warming smiles.

When Rosie had joined the local Brownie pack, she was allowed to help decorate the window behind the choir stalls. They had coloured little, cut-out roses, beautifully drawn by Brown Owl and these rainbow-like creatures now hung loosely along the sill, adding to the vision of colour that Brown Owl and Tawny Owl had created with the large rose blooms given generously by parents. They had been left in a bucket Brown Owl had placed on her doorstep, or had brought them willingly to the church that morning. These thoughtful gestures would be enjoyed by the local congregation on Sunday and the many visitors during the weekend. When she joined the other Brownies on Sunday morning, gathering in the church foyer, the scent was sweet and the vision of abundant soft petals welcomed the congregation. She liked singing the hymns and kneeling on the cushions, hidden from view as they listened to the prayers, although her mind wandered as she watched the other little girls making faces, whispering and fiddling with the books. She waved goodbye as they tumbled out of the church and she skipped down the road. They were going to lunch at Grandma and Grandad's as soon as she got back. They would be waiting for her.

Her grandparents had a good-sized terraced house in London, squeezed between two other identical houses, except for the individual features that stood out and made it easy for them to recognise, as they drove around the corner; it had a bright blue door and a large rhododendron growing under the grand bay window, framed by heavy, dark, ruby-coloured curtains. The front room was hidden to the world by the white lace-starched net curtains; pleats fell neatly in folds, depicting the care their gran gave to her home. The front door led to a long hallway with the back room to the left. The door at the end opened to a sitting room and small kitchen. A creaky staircase led from the hall, up to the bedrooms. The toilet was still outside; a wooden plank with a hole in it and a long chain to pull, that Rosie still struggled to reach. The potty under the bed was a novelty for the children, there only to use at night if they really needed to.

The regular fortnightly visits to the grandparents at the weekend were a constant in their lives but since their move, it took them just over an hour by car instead of the half an hour they were used to. They always got stuck in traffic at the busy roundabout not far from their grandparents' house, although coming home was quicker because it would be late. Rosie and Sam would be snuggled up under a blanket in their pyjamas, on the back seat of the car, fast asleep.

On their way to school on Monday, Rosie's mind was on her plan. "Come on, slowcoach, we'll be late!" Her brother pulled her eagerly, wanting to get to school to play with his friends. His energetic tug brought her out of her momentary thoughts... to the issue of her parents' holiday. She could picture them holding hands, enjoying a quiet and intimate moment, and felt sure this was a great idea. Looking down at the lovely little man in her care, she smiled and walked quicker.

"Would you like to go and stay at Grandma's?" she enquired. Sam tilted his head to one side before giving a definite "Yes!" His eagerness subsided for a cautious "Why?" and questionable "When?"

"Well, we'd have to ask Mum and Dad but I thought for half-term or during the Easter holidays, when there's no school," adding, "We could go to the park with the big slide and play in their garden and pick apples and play in Grandad's shed." Rosie listed as many favourite things as she could.

"Oh yes! Shall I ask Daddy if it's okay?"

"What a great idea," she replied, nodding – pleased with her manipulation of the small child. As they reached the school gates, a certain unnerving hesitation gripped her as she let go of her brother's hand and he ran off smiling and waving his little fist, clenched around the precious Dinky car he'd taken to school; his special 'something' to play with at 'toy time'. Rosie had felt the same nervousness around her brother on several occasions, a nervousness that something unhappy surrounded this little boy, but she could never decipher what it meant and would push such unpleasantries out of her mind to focus on the good. At this moment her pleasures revolved around her family, her grandparents and their love, as well as the thought of her parents' peace and happiness, feelings she felt very, very sure of.

Rosie had never known her mother's parents. They had both died a long time ago, before she was born. Her mother rarely talked about them. It was too painful. She did not need to, anyway. Rosie had her own pictures in her head. Marjorie loved Jim's parents as if they were her own. Although she was apprehensive about leaving the children behind, Rosie knew she was confident about giving such a responsibility to these two lovely people. There was no one else she would rather give the responsibility to.

Jim always wondered whether this particular holiday had been predestined, whether he had been fated to have the conversation that day with John, and wondered how much his cheeky, endearing daughter had been involved in instigating his and Marjorie's departure. Having deposited the two lively bundles at his mother's house in London, he watched them ushered into the garden to play hoopla with their grandad; six wooden curtain pole rings and a home-made wooden stick hammered into the ground at the end of the path, by the fence. This would provide entertainment for at least half an hour, while Marjorie drank tea with his mum and went over the logistics of looking after the children for a week.

"They'll be fine," she insisted. "Stop worrying. Just go off and enjoy yourselves, you deserve a holiday – so does Jim," she encouraged, wrapping an arm gently round her daughter-in-law's shoulder and smiling warmly at her son. Jim watched the two children at play, before thanking his dad and finishing his mug of tea and cake; Battenberg, his favourite, reminding him of his mum's thoughtfulness.

"Thank you again, Dad. I'm really looking forward to this break. I know Marjorie needs it, too… She's been a bit down lately."

"It's been a lot for her to take in: the move, the kids both at school, leaving her friends behind… she needs to find something to occupy her…and not just housework, eh?"

"Has Rosie or Marjorie said anything to you?" Jim asked, reacting to these words.

"No. Why?"

"Oh nothing – it's just Rosie's been on about her mum being unhappy and Marjorie mentioned college."

"Well, I think that makes a lot of sense. She would be doing something with that brain of hers, she's a clever lass…and she might even get a well-paid job so that you don't have to work so hard all the time…Anyway no need to think about that now. You go off and enjoy your holiday. And don't forget to take some pictures with that Polaroid John lent you." They shook hands and after a quick hug and kisses from their children, eager to return to their game, Marjorie and Jim climbed back into the Morris Minor and started the drive towards the airport.

Only last week, his brother John had phoned out of the blue to tell him about their great time in Tuscany. His new boss had a sister out there, Rosemary, and she had just started a bed and breakfast business with her husband Allen, in their newly renovated farmhouse. There was still a lot to do but they had focused on rebuilding the barn for rooms to let, to start bringing in some income. They were planning to retire there in a few months, when the business picked up. John and his wife had been invited to join his boss, Geoff, as their first guests, to try out one of the three apartments and to help them with the final finishes. John was a builder by trade, mainly plastering, plumbing and tiling, and his wife ran her own interior design business. They weren't short of money, the reward maybe for not having any children as a result of their business commitments. John had never wanted children anyway. The opportunity to work abroad for a couple of weeks and enjoy a holiday suited them.

Jim was fond of his brother, but they had very different lifestyles and they did not see much of each other now. John and his wife, Penny, were happy to play at being uncle and aunt to Jim's own children occasionally, though. The children liked the thought that their uncle was rich, and they thought Auntie Penny was amazing – beautiful, elegant and fun.

Jim happened to mention he was thinking of going on holiday with Marjorie, to have a break from the kids and work; that Mum and Dad were looking forward to having Rosie and Sam to stay, and John was quick to invite them to his boss's place in Italy.

"Don't be daft, we don't know them – he's your boss!" Jim felt a bit embarrassed that he'd mentioned the holiday because he felt like he'd almost invited himself. Now, of course, it seemed a strange coincidence.

"No, honestly," John enthused. "Look, I'll have a chat tomorrow and get him to ring you. They're such a lovely couple, I know you'll get on. Allen's a bit quiet but he works in England sometimes, flying to and from Italy so he might not be about. When he is there he can be a bit unsociable, preferring his own company, staying in his study most of the time, with his accounts. Great for a successful business, though," he said with an earnest sincerity. "When he does join his guests, though, he's great – likes his wine, too! Rosemary's dad, Stanley, is the social one and Geoff's sister, Rosemary, is quite a lot like your Marjorie." Jim was thinking his brother might mean, "boring, homely, not amazingly dynamic and glamorous like Penny", suddenly feeling guilty and irritated by his mental outburst.

"The more I think about it, the more it seems to make sense. Good job I rang really." He laughed confidently, and as Jim put the phone down with the usual slight irritation he felt after talking to his elder brother, he couldn't help but feel he had been totally controlled by those around him or by fate itself... But everything was falling into place effortlessly and he smiled. It would not be too expensive, just the flight for the two of them and whatever living costs the trip might entail. And abroad – Italy – wow, he wasn't expecting that!

CHAPTER 7

As they boarded the BOAC flight, Jim placed one hand protectively around Marjorie's waist, while handing their boarding passes to the neat, attractive air hostess with the other. Marjorie smiled nervously but excited at the prospect of travelling: she'd never flown before. Jim had only flown once, on business to Paris, for a couple of days the year before. He'd been slightly irritated by Marjorie's fussing in preparation for the trip; over the money, the packing and the children, but he was conscious of her nervousness about flying and going to a foreign country. She settled into her seat, safely secured with her seat belt tightened. Both looked eagerly out of the window, animated by the adventure they were embarking on.

The grey tarmac mingled with the grey sky, allowing a penetrating melancholy to shift momentarily into their thoughts. They sat silent for a while, watching the little truck being unloaded: various cases of differing browns and blacks being loaded beneath them, occasionally disturbed by a brighter piece of luggage. Neither of them were used to idle or meaningful chatter; it had been a while since they had conversed casually in each other's company. Jim spoke first, to express a thought that had been nagging him for a while, breaking the silence.

"Rosie's a quiet one, don't you think?"

"What do you mean?"

"You know…thoughtful…knowing…"

Marjorie looked more closely at Jim, surprised by such an interest in the children and alerted by his perceptive comment. She wondered whether her own concerns were replicated by others, and now she felt an engaging bond suddenly with the man she knew she loved but had felt quite distant to of late.

"I thought I was the only one who had noticed." She leant towards him in an almost conspiratorial manner.

"Not just quiet and thoughtful, she seems to know things, not like a psychic or anything, but just what's right or what will help. I have no idea where she gets all her goodness from." Unsure of her own husband's thoughts, she added, "Do you find it irritating?"

"Oh no… just special, I suppose." They looked at each other a little alarmed at such a conversation about their daughter and then Jim leant back and laughed:

"We're just a couple of very lucky and very proud parents."

"I think she just seems so good because Sam is such a little scamp!" They smiled comfortably in their joint parental amusement and let their attention drift outside the window once more, any concerns that had been building up dissipating in a shared agreement of understanding. A dormant warmth surfaced and settled as Jim reached out and squeezed Marjorie's hand gently.

John's boss, Geoff, had returned to England, back to work and back to help John complete an important deal. He was confident that this client John was close to securing would make the company quite a lot of money. Allen was still in London. Although he had retired from his job in the bank, he still had a few clients who relied on his financial advice. He also had the house to sell. He wasn't quite ready to move to Italy full-time and enjoyed the buzz of living in the city as much as the serenity of the Tuscan rolling hills. The villa was Rosemary's dream more than his, but Allen was happy if she was happy, and they were fairly independent of each other.

Rosemary had been living in Italy with her father, Stanley, for almost two months now. They were working on advertising the apartments in the farmhouse with a local holiday company. They already had links with a tour operator in England, keen to obtain such an exclusive and pretty holiday property. The fact that Marjorie's father-in-law was also called Stanley seemed to be a good sign. As they ventured through the departure gates, she spotted a kindly gent scouring the visitors and settling his eyes on her. He gave her a saucy wink, holding a card with their names written on. She waved back like an excited schoolgirl, grinning in acknowledgement. That must be Stanley.

The drive from Pisa Airport took just over an hour. The conversation was generally about the property, about its dilapidated state when they first acquired it, which had gradually been transformed into an hospitable retreat. It still needed some work to parts of the house and to the garden, but Rosemary was enjoying digging, planting and searching for ornamental pots and statues to plant in the more prominent areas around the grounds. The pool they had built was Rosemary's pride and joy, and she was hoping that Marjorie would help her choose some more shrubs to adorn the grassed area surrounding it. She had already placed a couple of stone statues, depicting Bacchus and Cupid and three terracotta urns, which now required some trailing begonias or similar colourful plants.

The roads became narrower and it seemed to Jim that they were venturing out into the middle of nowhere. He felt a sense of anxiety at being so far off from the beaten track, but tried to enjoy the surroundings with a positive sense of adventure. Marjorie was gazing out of the window, with a sense of awe and delight, dreamily absorbing the most inviting and idyllic scenery she had ever seen. Rectangles of small trees, with delicate, grey-green leaves, Stanley informed her, provided the olives for the oil that was made locally – something Rosemary hoped to make from the many trees they had inherited with the land they had procured. The regimental rows and rows of climbing plants held the luscious grapes which would provide the wonderful Chianti Marjorie would inevitably acquire a taste for in the coming week.

As they pulled up in front of the stone-built building, at the end of a rather bumpy gravel track which seemed to lead nowhere, Marjorie and Jim looked fondly at each other. The romantic backdrop to this farmhouse, of hills, green cypresses and vineyards stretching out as far as they could see, was met halfway by the rich, azure sky, reaching up and flooding the horizon as it fought with the heated haze. This was more than they had ever hoped for.

Later, after they had satisfied their hosts with an animated reception, Marjorie and Jim unpacked and made themselves at home in the beautiful, though rather sparse Tuscan apartment. Marjorie went to help Rosemary in the kitchen, preparing the seafood and antipasto for a typically Tuscan meal, while Stanley lit up the neatly built barbeque pit, to cook the large steaks and sausages. Jim stood aside, sipping his first glass of Italian wine, and watched the older man. For a moment he felt a deep and heartfelt glow and he thought of Rosie – this was her doing and the image of her smiling warmly up at him penetrated his thoughts. As he visualised her sweet face, he dreamt he could hear her say: "How lovely...Love you, Dad."

The balmy evening was a gentle start to their holiday, as the four of them sat around the large, marble-topped table, talking idly about the Italian lifestyle, building horror stories and local exploits. Marjorie and Jim talked mostly of the children, in a leisurely tone that made it evident that they were missed. They stood finally, and retired to their room, the warmth of the wine and the night's heat tempting them to bed.

The next morning they were enticed by the large, rectangular pool shimmering and blinking in the heat. They settled on the sunbeds acquired thoughtfully by Rosemary for their holiday, and admired the pool stretched out beside them. They enjoyed the first couple of days' experiences with spoilt abandonment, discussing plans and ideas with their newfound companions, who continually encouraged them to relax in these peaceful and idyllic surroundings. Today, Jim was lying in a quiet, sun-induced stupor. In the far corner, the concrete statue waited, perched on the red-tiled walkway. He lazily gazed at the figure – a young goddess delicately robed, offering a shell shyly to an invisible audience.

Marjorie had gone with Rosemary into the local village to look at plants and have coffee. It had been too hot for her: she felt tired and was missing the children. Jim had felt irritated by this and snapped unkindly, "Why do you always have to moan and complain?" Unsettled by his outburst, she had decided to take up Rosemary's offer for a visit to the local shops. Yesterday by the pool he'd rolled over onto his front and ignored her as she reached for her towel and sunglasses and went to give him an apologetic kiss, missing him as he turned away and feeling sadly abandoned. She had walked off quickly to the coolness of the room, with quiet tears. Today she decided to give him some space and amuse herself with her newfound friend.

As Jim lay back and remembered his behaviour towards his wife yesterday, he now felt guilty. His behaviour towards Marjorie bothered him. He pulled himself up to sip the water, glancing again at the statue of the young goddess, momentarily disturbed by its presence. Her head seemed to move in the haze. Assured by his senses that this was a heat-related vision under half-opened eyelids, he allowed himself to be absorbed, floating mindlessly in this strange, dreamlike state. The movement was ignored, but a more obvious turning of the stone head, gentle but defined, caught his eye again and as she faced him, she blinked. The imaginary tales from books, films and television dramas, of gods and humans involved in great feats of wonder and adventure, crossed his mind but this was a quiet, quizzical confrontation between a cold, hard statue of artistic taste and a rambling, heat-absorbed brain relaxing in a pensive mood. He looked more alertly but the moment had gone. He lay back to let his mind wander in an effortless sleep, but the image of the figure had engaged his conscience.

Much later, it seemed, he sat up, and looked towards

the apartment. Turning to glance at the robed statue, his mood softened and for some reason he winked back. As he turned back, he imagined Marjorie returning, draped in a robe. She turned her head and offered him not a shell, but a cool glass of water with ice. He realised then that it was Marjorie...and she was back. Unsettled, confused, he realised he must have fallen into a deep sleep because, as he glanced at his watch, several hours had lapsed. He seemed to have lost all sense of time.

"I'm sorry. It's the heat. I think it makes me irritable." Marjorie spoke first.

"It seems to be having an effect on me, too," he offered, taking the water.

Whether it was the heat or a sudden thought of Rosie, he suddenly felt himself aroused. The fact that they seemed completely alone for once allowed him to lean towards his wife and kiss her passionately. Then he whispered, "I love you, Marjorie." Her heart leapt at his words. She responded immediately, kissing him fondly on the mouth. The rest of the holiday was like a romantic honeymoon and when they piled the cases in the car for the return home, Marjorie suddenly felt a pang of guilt that she had not missed the children once in the last few days.

On their return, the hustle of the London traffic stimulated Jim and Marjorie's senses, climatising them with the stable diet of a busy day and a forced working energy. The rows of terraced houses, doors hiding a hub of activity or desertion until 'home time', replaced the green landscapes and the holiday heat which became more like a dream every day. The idyllic calm of the Tuscan summer was seeping slowly from their relaxed, sun-tanned bodies and the timeless experience faded into a well-formed memory to be indulged in during other calmer, future times.

CHAPTER 8

The front door flung open to welcome them in: a small, smiling soldier, waving his cardboard sword valiantly, ran towards them.

"Mummy, Mummy, I'm a soldier. Grandad made me some armour and everything…" Marjorie gathered him up and smothered him in kisses. He leant over with his arms stretched out towards his daddy.

"Look, Daddy, look." His neediness was reciprocated with a firm grip as his father swung him into the air and placed him on his shoulders.

"Mind his head!" Rosie called as her father strolled towards the looming door frame, Sam towering above. Jim ducked just in time, casually patting her head as he passed.

"We missed you, sweetheart," he crooned. "And yes, we had a lovely time – all is good." He smiled and winked lightly at her, suddenly seized by the memory of the statue.

They sat comfortably around the table, the adults drinking cups of tea in Grandma's favourite bone china tea set. A delicate pink flower ordained the teacup and saucer against a pale blue background, the rim touched with a delicate, golden edge. Rosie loved and admired the beauty

Rosie's Gift

of such craftmanship and felt very grown up when she was finally allowed to hold and use the much-loved crockery. A few years later, the occasion had not been a happy one. Just now they drank Robinsons orange squash from the sturdy beakers that were purchased especially for them at the local corner shop, from Mrs Smith, the lady who wore a silk scarf on her head and had a big bosom. Granny would spend ages talking to her over the counter about her neighbours, their families and their constant domestic dramas. Everyone knew everyone, it seemed, and there was always a story to be told. There was no need for *EastEnders* in those days, although *Coronation Street* was becoming a firm favourite on Grandma's new black and white television – after *The Archers*, on the radio, of course.

Grandma's coffee cake was a speciality, large walnut halves positioned carefully and neatly onto the creamy and sugary coffee coating on top, with more cream oozing out from the middle. Sam's sticky fingers clutched another handful, and he crammed it in with another hungry mouthful.

"That's enough, you'll make yourself sick," his mother warned pointlessly.

"He's fine, a growing boy – and a great little soldier, eh, Sam?" his grandfather added.

"Yes, Grandpa," he grinned, giving him a warm response and gathering up his sword again to take aim at the chair next to him.

71

"Watch out!" Too late, the vase was falling but Rosie had caught it, as expected, and everyone was laughing at his antics. There was never anything malicious with Sam, just his clumsy, excited energy, and Rosie's adeptness often saved the day. This was a wonderful family moment, another to treasure.

As the evening wore on, the children retired exhausted to the little single bed they shared upstairs in the second bedroom, fitting themselves uncomfortably in the limited space but warmed by the closeness that continued to grow between brother and sister. Mummy and Daddy would sneak up quietly later, when darkness and sleepiness had smothered them. The adults spent the evening playing cards and chatting around the table.

"Sam has found himself a new little friend, you know," Stanley announced as he laid down the Ace of Hearts.

"Yes, little Paul from number 5. He stays with his aunt while his mum's away. He's a bit older, but very sweet," Sylvia added.

"Sam's always been friendly," Marjorie mused.

"And what about Rosie?"

"Oh, she's just lovely, reading and colouring mostly, but we've been cooking together and chatting – and her knitting is coming along. Did I show you the jumper I'm knitting for Sam?" She leant down and pulled a bright yellow knitted rectangle from the cotton bag, a gentle clatter of needles at the bottom, moved as she placed the bag down. There was a short pause in the game as the women regarded her work, then Sylvia picked up her cards and, swapping one card for the Queen of Diamonds, looked up from the deck and declared:

"Rummy!"

The four of them continued to enjoy their stories from the week before, varying the card games from 'Sevens', 'Whist', 'Rummy' and 'Newmarket', the cards spaced evenly over the velvety-green tablecloth, the twisted wool fringes hanging softly over the side of the table, the ones that tickled your bare knees in the summer. Eventually tiredness encouraged them to retire to bed. The large bed with the heavy oyster eiderdown waited for Marjorie and Jim as the children drifted silently in their world of sleep to the steady echoing tick-tock of the clock on the mantelpiece. They would leave in the morning for home. Jim was thoughtful: a wonderful holiday, an enjoyable couple of days with his mum and dad, and now home, to rebuild what had been crumbling for a few years, to secure with new cement the foundations of their marriage and their love. No one ever knew about his indiscretion with the young secretary Lucy, before they moved, but a twinge of regret now nagged at him and he turned over to kiss the wife he might have lost with such foolishness.

Sam's friendship with Paul began to grow. Every time they visited his grandparents, Sam would go around to see him.

The family enjoyed a few hours of peace, sometimes having to pick him up on their way home because he had forgotten the time. Paul would be invited to dinner now and again, so that Sylvia and Stanley got to see him. Paul enjoyed the roast dinners. He and his aunt rarely enjoyed the luxury. She was often working or too tired to be in the kitchen cooking. A fish and chip takeaway or beans on toast was a regular meal in their household.

He and Sam would play Subbuteo in the front room after they had eaten, or watch the football on the black and white television with Stanley and Jim. The women would sit at the table after they had cleaned away and drink tea, knit or do the crossword in the Sunday paper. Later they would all play cards. This was a new pastime for Paul. They patiently taught him the rules and he joined in until his aunt rang. Paul preferred just hanging out with Sam because he felt rather awkward amidst a family setting. He was used to his own company, the quiet company of his aunt, or the more lively company of a few mates, hanging about near the corner shop.

CHAPTER 9

It was quiet in the house that Saturday morning. Sam was watching his dad reading the paper at the kitchen table, pretending to read his book, copying his father's mannerisms with an endearing, thoughtful silence. Marjorie was washing the dishes, her hands gently kissed by the Fairy bubbles in the sink, and Rosie sat in the hall, writing a poem for school. It was one of those peaceful moments that might be captured on an iPhone today, but in the 1970s it was just a simple moment that would be etched into their memories and held close, like an old friend.

Rosie began to fidget uncomfortably and looked up towards the kitchen. She moved from the hall slowly and stood in the doorway, facing her mother nervously; a nagging, unpleasant ache was growing. She recognised the feeling and knew it meant trouble. A sudden need to hold her grandfather close, to tell him she loved him and to see him, took over all her senses. She tried to speak casually but she knew her words would create alarm – her mother was well aware by now of her 'gifts', as she called them.

"Mum?" It was questioning enough for her mother to turn to her, speculatively, and put the pan down that she was holding. She looked attentively at her twelve-year-old daughter.

"What is it, darling?" Rosie paused, inviting a more focused response from her mum, who had wiped her hands gently but purposefully on the tea towel, before asking:

"Shall we go into the living room?"

Jim rustled the newspaper, aware of their movements and gentle murmurings, but eager to remain removed from the conversation. As a family they had grown to understand the value of Rosie's insight and avoided drama or speculation. She was a beautiful child and they were sensitive to her needs and wishes. Only good had ever come from her insights, however unnerving these manifestations seemed to be. Sam was insensitive to most things which did not involve food or play and he never really understood or liked this side of his sister. He had been teased about her on occasions at school, saying that she was "Alright, I suppose – for a sister", or dismissing his relationship with comments such as, "That's the problem with girls!" He felt at a loss when he considered his real thoughts and feelings. He loved her, she was his sister after all, but she was a bit strange and all that 'goodness' often got on his nerves.

Sam preferred to be out with his mates, on his bike or kicking a ball against the garage doors, until some old biddy came and shouted at them to "Go away!" His trips to London were great, his grandad was ace, and his grandma cooked great food: yummy cakes and Angel Delight. His best mate Paul was always at his aunt's now, and he'd wander down the road, almost as soon as he arrived at his grandparents', to Paul's auntie's house, a few doors up. Theirs was only a small, two-bedroomed terrace, but it was big enough for the two boys to lark about in. Mostly they played with an old racing game that his aunt had bought at a jumble sale. The metal horses were on a cord, threaded through them, which, when pulled on, would move them forward. The harder you pulled, the quicker they galloped along the table. If you pulled too hard, they toppled over and you had to start again. It was a simple toy but brought delight and friendly arguments to the lively pair, who loved the competition and challenge. Sometimes they sat playing cards, Snap mainly; it was easy and they could shout a lot, but most of the time they would mess about at the park. Sometimes his aunt was out and they'd run around the house and help themselves to anything they could find. Paul's Auntie Julie was often busy or out. Paul never seemed to talk about his mum and Sam never thought to ask. Paul had mentioned her boyfriend once, with some unpleasantness, complaining that he never saw her anymore and "It's all his fault!" But Sam's fleeting interest was quickly consumed with other interests.

Rosie and her mum sat comfortably on the sofa and Rosie began.

"Is Grandad alright, Mum?"

Marjorie was immediately alarmed and her concern

showed. He had gone into hospital to have a gallstone removed, but it didn't seem to be anything to worry about. He was only 60 years old and he'd had one removed before; no one had seemed particularly concerned. The children hadn't been told because it seemed an unnecessary worry for them that they wouldn't really understand. No one was worried – except, suddenly, Rosie.

"I want to see him and tell him how much I love him." She realised she was crying, warm tears spread on her cheeks. Noticing her soft sadness, her mother held her close, feeling her own panic rise. A fear began to grip her like a vice. She knew Rosie. She understood her deep, intuitive words and got up gently.

"We will all go and see him this evening." Her daughter smiled warmly and her voice lightened.

"Thank you, Mum."

They had a solid and secure bond because she was 'special', and as they hugged each other, satisfied, they returned to the kitchen. Just now no fuss was made. The family followed and believed Rosie's heartfelt requests, reassured by her convictions and suggestions, but today she felt alarmed. Rosie could hear her mother and father talking quietly in the hall. Jim's voice was suddenly louder and urgent. Marjorie had not managed to contact her mother-in-law and Jim's further efforts were fruitless, too, just the constant 'beep beep' on the end of the line, indicating no one was at home. While they were discussing what to do, Sylvia rang. Stanley had collapsed suddenly and had been rushed by ambulance to Greenwich Hospital.

The drive was melancholy and it seemed to take longer than usual. They drove up and down the rows, looking aimlessly for somewhere to park. So many cars for a small car park. London suddenly felt uninviting and overpeopled. They stopped and started scouring the area for a space, feeling a frustrating urgency. Moving, finally, into a vacated place, they climbed out of the vehicle and scurried across the walkway towards the large doors of the hospital entrance.

The doors banged shut behind them as they moved methodically, with an overhanging silence; even Sam was quiet today. Moving unnaturally slowly, Sam was aware of the clicking noise his shoes made on the tiles. He loved his grandad and expected him to live forever; well, at least until he was all grown up – not now – he wasn't supposed to leave him now. Jim and Marjorie held hands for comfort and reassurance. Rosie and Sam did the same. At the end of the corridor and up two flights of stairs, their father paused before pushing open the doors into the ward. They opened to reveal a row of metal, prison-like beds, divided by large, brown plastic chairs, some occupied by a visitor, some waiting empty, anticipating loved ones who would not be coming.

It was hard to find Stanley: the beds were filled with old men, looking tired, some wired up or comatose with drugs inducing sleep. Rosie knew where to find him. She walked to the next cubicle and made her way to the bed in the right-hand corner, where her dear grandfather lay – also asleep. A tube was running from his hand up to a transparent bag, towering over a small table beside him. The little, shrunken man, pale and barely recognisable to the children, was clinging to life. The family had followed her to his bedside and Sylvia hugged them, rising slowly from the brown plastic chair beside her husband.

Marjorie wept and took Sam's hand to guide him to the shop while Jim had a moment with his mother and father. Rosie was left standing at the end of the bed, dealing with her own grief. She had her hug: she told Grandad Stanley that she loved him and that was all she could do. Stanley opened his eyes weakly and looked first at his wife, then his son, and then finally he turned to Rosie. As he looked knowingly at his granddaughter, she moved in closer to hear his whispers; to hear what he had to say.

"Thank you for getting the family here." There was a short pause before he spoke again. "It's a gift." Sylvia reached forward and squeezed his hand.

"Tell her, Sylvia, later, tell her later…" Jim could see him struggling.

"Shh, Dad, rest now," and he turned away to hide the tears he could not control. Marjorie was back with Sam and they stood and watched this wonderful man falling quietly back into a deathly sleep. Marjorie strengthened her resolve and moved towards him, "Oh Stanley... Dad," she whispered, and the solemn family watched him quietly.

A nurse arrived to usher three of them away. "Only two visitors at a time, I'm afraid." Jim took Sam and Rosie out into the corridor and to the waiting room, his footsteps reluctant and heavy. Rosie moved slowly beside him and Sam swung his arms nervously and restlessly, following behind.

Jim looked at his daughter thoughtfully and asked tentatively, "Isn't there anything you could have done – you know – did you see anything?" She knew what he was suggesting. Why have a gift if you cannot use it to save a loved one?

"No, I'm sorry, Dad, it was his time. There was – there is nothing anyone can do. It's just his time," she repeated. They sat in silence, nursing their grief until Marjorie arrived.

The journey back to what was now Sylvia's home was held in a silent vacuum. It would become a place of grief for a while, as she wandered around it aimlessly, looking and listening pointlessly for Stanley, in the middle of the night, when she would wake fretfully and find herself lost in the house she'd always lived in. But friends and her family eased her into a life without the man she still loved. It was a massive heart attack that had taken Stanley from them that winter. It was a great loss to the family, but her grandfather's words to Sylvia, "Tell her, tell her later", resonated in Rosie's mind.

As they sat deep in conversation, one afternoon – Sam was playing in the back room with his Subbuteo and her parents had gone for a walk – Sylvia opened up with words which had been hidden for a long time.

"As your Grandad Stanley told you, it's a gift, Rosie, darling – a gift." She moved nearer as if to reveal some huge secret. "Your grandfather had some of it when he was young. It saved him from a few scrapes in the war – not that he liked to ever talk about it much. His mother had it, too. She used to tell fortunes. I'm not sure about before her. Of course it would have been considered witchcraft in the olden days." Rosie gazed with new and knowing eyes at this little old lady – her grandmother – who had always been so ordinary – now engaged in a conversation that would bring them closer, closer than they had ever been.

"Look after your gift – it is unpredictable, coming and going or lost forever. Take care, love," and she bent down so she could kiss her gently on the cheek.

Up until now, Rosie had only sensed what was right, what she "just knew". She had recently read about Joan of Arc at school and she had been reminded of Paul's conversion on the road to Damascus in assembly, but they were just stories, similar to the tales she had heard as a little girl, of miracles, of saints and uncanny coincidences or superstitions, her thoughts and 'voices', were subtle. She avoided situations with friends that would cause upset, and guided others with a gentle persuasive ease to help them. One time at school the teacher had asked them all to learn a poem. She was going to ask one or two of them to recite it the next day and the teacher told them if they could not recite it properly, they would miss their break and have to write it out ten times. Rosie had known somehow that David would be asked. He never did his work and hated learning things. Rosie waited at the door to catch him as he left.

"David, I know she's going to ask you to recite the poem tomorrow. I heard her tell Mr Smith in the corridor that she wanted to test you." She added the white lie at the end to cover herself and make the story sound plausible. David's face crumpled. The frown left small wrinkles on his forehead. He muttered something. The next day he'd learnt the poem satisfactorily enough for Mrs Harris's approval and surprise, and everyone clapped. Rosie knew that meant a lot to him. He worked much harder after that, seeking similar praise. Even Mrs Harris began to like him for his improved attitude. Rosie was drawn to the front of the class, where she was forming an image of a much older David, this time talking to the students in front of him as a grown man, a teacher, she realised, and she smiled contentedly.

Today she heard it quite clearly at the tea table, a voice of her own, a voice so clear she turned around in alarm.

"This is important – listen to me – follow these feelings", and with those words she saw her dad and felt a tumultuous pain throbbing alarmingly in her head.

Both her mother and father were aware that something had startled her and was now drawing her attention away from the sausages and mash in front of her. They had both become more watchful of her quiet moods. The blinding ray of morning sunshine was licking at her father's shoes and for a moment Rosie's eyes watched it, as if trying to receive some sort of message.

"Is something bothering you?" her father asked. The voice had dissipated into a lulling murmur and Rosie blushed as if caught doing something wrong.

"No – I am sorry. I thought I heard someone but it must have been my imagination again." Then more bravely added:

"I don't want you to go to work yet, Daddy," and, suddenly overwhelmed, ran from the room in tears.

Jim was not overly alarmed and usually remained fairly casual about her unusual outbursts, but this time he picked up the phone with a controlled determination and rang his office number.

"Hi, Mac, it's Jim. Sorry, mate, but I'm running a bit late today – kids – you know what it's like…yeah, Okay…see you later." He turned and looked through the open door, towards the stairs and sighed; not a sad or bored sigh, but one of concern and love. He found her, cradled into a foetal position, grasping her covers for comfort, as he entered the room.

A gentle line of brightness entered through the crack in the curtains, which had been pulled across in a frantic gesture, dramatically shutting out the world. A rainbow of colours spread across the pale cream carpet, like a beam of magic. Dull shadows immersed the rest of the room into a darkened state of mystery as Jim sat heavily on the small bed and reached out, taking hold of her hot hand.

"Now, what's all this about, my little princess?"

The telephone rang downstairs, disturbing their quiet, intimate and sensitive moment. No words had been spoken as her father gently flicked the hair back that was bothering her eyes, wiping her tears away, lightly, with his hanky.

"It's okay now." She spoke with a renewed energy, the tension noticeably lifting. She raised her head from the dampened pillow and smiled softly. "I'm glad you stayed," in a stronger and more confident voice adding, "you'd better answer the phone and get off to work."

Jim replaced the receiver – slowly.

"Shit!" His exclamation was caught emphatically by Marjorie, "Jim!"

"There's been an accident, three or four cars at least, two fatalities, they think. That was Mac. He was checking I hadn't left yet." There was a stunned silence. Jim moved forward and put his arms round Marjorie, holding her tight, holding on to engage some sense of what had happened and control the unstable emotions he felt, realising the significance of what he had just heard.

"My God, Marjorie, Rosie might just have saved my life. If I had left just ten minutes earlier..." His wife couldn't speak. She clung to him, an attempt to calm her shaking hands. She felt sick, relieved and then thoughtful.

Upstairs, Rosie got up and finished getting ready for school, her thoughts now engaged on the task of packing her bag. She liked her secondary school. She particularly liked her English teacher, Mrs Sanderson. She talked with a firm but kind voice and often praised Rosie for her work. She had several pieces of work on the wall. In her last year at primary school, she had Mrs Harris, who was unkind to the boys who struggled with the work or spoke when she had told them to be silent. Sam had her this year and his hands would often be sore from being smacked with the wooden ruler she kept on her desk. Rosie had taught Sam some tricks to stay quiet; he needed to look at the board or teacher as if he was interested, even if he was not, and let his mind wander to things he liked doing and then try to repeat in his mind some of the things she said, as a sort of distraction and to provide some sort of answer, should she ask him a random question. She would also help him with his work at home so that he could avoid being punished so unfairly.

Last year he had Mrs Lyons and he was doing really well with his reading, writing and maths. This year his studies seemed to deteriorate. Mrs Lyons offered an extra class at lunchtime for those who needed extra help but Sam was too busy running around the playground to bother. Rosie kept him out of trouble as much as she could. It was only for a year and then he would be leaving to join her at the high school.

CHAPTER 10

Rosie had been nearly eleven years old when her mother began to study. Sam was now causing boisterous havoc at school and she was often too distracted these days by essays and deadlines she needed to meet, to notice. When the leaflet had been pushed through the letter box, about courses at the local college starting in September, Jim and Marjorie had settled on the sofa to seriously consider the financial implications and options open to her. Sam, quietly playing upstairs with his Subbuteo, was ignorant of his parents' needs. As long as he was fed and not asked to do too much, he was generally content. Rosie was more aware and often watchful, although she tried not to interfere.

"I'm just going up to see if Sam's okay," she offered, as much to herself as to them. Her parents looked up and smiled, returning to the discussion about her studies with simple consideration. Sam was engrossed with his little Subbuteo figures, surrounded by the usual scattered mess of clothes and paper which was associated with his bedroom. He was developing a new technique with the tiny football figurines, flicking the base at an angle to secure enough skill that he could beat his dad and his friends, Nick and Tony. He had begun to amuse himself with numbers and calculations as a manager. He was bright and numerate for his age, Rosie thought, as she stood watching him. Aware of her presence, he glanced up.

"Do you want to play?" he asked, delighted by the thought that this was something he could beat his sister at.

"Alright. Which team am I?" Sam gave her the team dressed in a smart, blue-striped kit, as Liverpool or Arsenal were more to his liking and one of the blue players had a hand missing; the deformity suggested a weakness, although he rolled and moved just as adeptly as the other little men on the pitch. He enjoyed these moments with his sister. The dull murmurings of his parents didn't interest him, and his sister was no challenge with his games. If she was beating him, she would allow him to win in the end. It was a pleasant change for her to have her head out of a book; she was always reading. "Just let me finish reading this chapter…" was a regular reply for his request for assistance, although he rather enjoyed the fact that she seemed to know when he really needed help or felt bored and she was very generous, finding time to amuse him when he really needed company and not just when he was feeling awkward or demanding. He was mostly amused by his own naughtiness but admired the way she was never riled by his irritating behaviour. He was just "being a boy", a term thrown his way on many occasions.

After almost half an hour, Rosie made some excuse and ventured downstairs: her mother, she knew, would be keen to ask her what she thought about the choices she was going to make. As she entered the lounge, her mother looked across the room towards her.

"What do you think, Rosie?" Rosie was aware of the weighted question and answered economically and casually, "Teaching is a great idea and I think you will enjoy the English and Art A Levels. I'm not so sure about Mathematics, though, it will be very hard. What about Geography? You are interested in people and the environment." And that was that – the decision was made.

The day she started college was very liberating. Rosie had enjoyed the last year of primary school, confidently in charge of her brother, and she was enjoying the activities school had to offer. She would even wait and watch over Sam, when he had football practice after school. The boys would run around, following the ball excitably; what they lacked in structure they gained with enthusiasm. Sam's visits to his grandmother's prevented him from playing regularly for the local football team but this did not bother him too much. He enjoyed a kick-around in the park, but he was not committed enough to join a football team. His mother did not always visit his grandparents at the weekend these days, which gave her time to work on her notes and essays. Her daughter would sometimes stay at home, too, completely committed to her own schooling, and this gave Marjorie further encouragement. Now Rosie was at secondary school, they would both settle down to homework with an enthusiastic relish for their studies.

The death of their grandfather had affected them badly for a while. Sam had become strangely quiet and reflective at home and excitable at school. He entertained his mates at school with his mischievous and comical behaviour, partly seeking attention, partly distraction from any emotions that bothered him. Rosie had taken to reading in her bedroom or helping her father enthusiastically in the garden and garage, feeling guilty for not being able to warn him or prevent the death of his father. But, as children often do, they moved on with their lives, focusing on their friends, school and the weekends, which would provide them with the freedom of games in the garden and bike rides to the park or picnics down by the river.

For her father, time with his family had become more precious; he spent less time at work and more time at weekends in London, with his mother. Sam would often travel with him to spend a few hours with his friend Paul. His grandma was pleased to see him briefly, but she was often distracted with her own thoughts and he knew she was very sad. Sam did not really know what to say. He would make her cups of tea and watch her knit before going down the road to Paul's house, leaving his father to tidy the garden and potter around the place doing odd jobs his own father used to do, with his father's tools. It gave Jim some comfort and he knew his mum liked him being around. He tried to persuade her to move nearer to them, but her reply was always the same:

"I've lived all my life in this house; I was born in this house and I will die in this house!"

She missed Stanley every day but her knitting and the neighbours kept her company most of the time.

It was a rather damp Wednesday morning. Marjorie had lectures all day. It would be taxing, but she loved engrossing herself in her studies and forgetting her motherly duties for a while. She was driven by the need to establish some sort of future beyond motherhood and wifely household duties.

Sitting in the classroom, with the fifteen other keen students, most of whom seemed so much cleverer than her, Marjorie leant back in her chair and smiled to herself. She paused to scan through her scribbles, a quiet relapse from the concentration involved, as she listened to the lecturer, who was beginning to ramble. She wished he would get back to the narrative and the characterisations in *King Lear*, rather than the more confusing intricacies of the language. She enjoyed the sound of the rhythm and the irony of the foreboding words spoken, but his references to the classical terms and to other writers was more difficult to follow, and at this precise moment, her notes were becoming erratic and repetitive; she was struggling to keep up and felt her words would not be particularly helpful when she read them back. The notes he had provided would hopefully make more sense when she read them through again later. His tedious, monotonal rendition of an essay he was referring to, in front of him, was not helping.

She'd hoped Rosie might be able to help her with her studies: she always seemed so capable and knowing, but it was a ridiculous notion, she thought, to assume her eleven-year-old daughter would be able to help her with such academic questions. Whenever a decision was made, Marjorie would seek guidance from her daughter. Although she knew it was rather annoying, Rosie would always provide a helpful suggestion, in a straightforward manner, without any fuss – and that suggestion was always adhered to.

Rosie was focusing more on her studies at school now. Her teenage years were made more enjoyable by her own friendships with Sarah from next door and Jackie at school, as well as her quite regular visits to her Auntie Penny. There was a happy and contented atmosphere around the Birch household.

CHAPTER 11

Although their wonderful holiday in Tuscany had brought John and Jim closer, their lives were very different. More recently they had seen less of them as Penny and John were travelling again and enjoying their 'freedom', as Jim saw it, with slight envy. They loved idling in the sun. They could afford it. They had no children. Jim smiled contentedly. His family meant more than any holiday.

Penny floated in the sea, bobbing weightlessly, the silky waves rippling generously around her, white edges flicking over the rim of the waves as they neared the beach. The blueness of the sky reflected on the clear water as she looked down at her feet, moving just above the sand beneath. Looking up, she took in the haze of the horizon, the mountains, dotted with green; trees like a carpet of shrubs in the distance, varied, thick and then sparse, against the mountainous cream rock, contrasting with the blue backdrop with the occasional white wisps of cloud gently moving towards the sea. A line travelled halfway up the hills, dotted with mainly white vehicles, flowing smoothly along at regular intervals.

She turned gracefully in the water to look behind, to

the open sea and the white sails travelling in the distance, similar to the vehicles but slower, more majestic and free. This is how she felt at that moment, free: the vast ocean stretched out before her, welcoming her body in its rhythmic, swaying beat, allowing her senses to take control, allowing her mind to wander.

As she turned again towards the beach, she scoured the view. Small children squealed as their feet and hands splashed at the water's edge. Older children kicked in abandoned play or threw balls to each other, running and splashing in and out of the sea; parents and grandparents slept, watched the delighted children at play or read, engrossed in their own delights on this sun-drenched shore. John was also reading. She had homed in on their established 'spot' on the beach. He must have sensed her watchful gaze and waved. Penny waved back automatically. There was a warm, steady understanding of love...but now in her forties, she had come to realise that their love was much more of a convenient comfort than the passionate, lustful love she now felt emerging every time she met Geoff, John's boss. He had these sexy blue eyes...a rather small nose...but his eyes... She distracted herself, momentarily regaining her composure, as she took in the sparkling reflection of the sun on the sea.

The waves moved in the same thoughtful rhythm of her inner thoughts. She conjured up visions: his eyes, his smile and her reflective fancies. She allowed her body to swim naturally and in time with the sea. She didn't want a sordid affair to mess up her life, her contentment but... She lay her head back into the sea, drifting aimlessly, eyes closed against the sun, losing herself to the heat, trying not to think now, not to disturb the pleasure, the freedom, of this moment.

Penny pushed her way out of the clutches of the sea, her sinking feet encased in the sand, the forceful current washing her back in, when it got the chance. She wondered whether it was the softness underfoot that made her progress so slowly, or reluctance to join society – and her husband. She looked with interest at his greying hair and broad shoulders, considering their love as she dried herself and draped herself with the towel, sitting back into the beach chair. While John absorbed himself with the words of Ian Fleming, unravelling another crime, she closed her eyes to indulge herself further with her thoughts and imaginings.

After their return, normal routines resumed. The smooth stability of life was reassuring, like an anchor for her rather tumultuous behaviour and contrary thoughts. Tonight, Penny was meeting Sue. They were going clubbing. She enjoyed this freedom, too, while John sat at his desk, contemplating discerning issues regarding his construction company. He did a lot less manual work now, in fact he had talked about selling the business; retiring early, enjoying travelling more and maybe buying a little place abroad, France or Italy maybe; a project to 'do up'. He was nearly 50 and seeking a challenge. Penny was not really part of that challenge, although he very much wanted her to be.

Her mind wandered towards sentiments of her small family – John's family – imaginings and wistful thoughts becoming a constant in her life these days. Rosie was going to secondary school next week and she'd taken her shopping to get her uniform. Marjorie had some reading to complete for college. She was very generous with Rosie, allowing Penny to be a special aunt, a second 'mother'. Penny knew Marjorie believed she had missed out by not having children – and perhaps she had…but she and John had enjoyed their life, their independence, their freedom, and when she had considered, briefly, the idea of having children, time had passed her by. A guilty feeling heckled her now; she wasn't enjoying life as much now. She didn't feel trapped, but she did seek more freedom and independence.

Although John was enjoying perusing over the figures for his next venture, an exciting transformation of an old cottage neglected by the old lady who had recently passed away, he had thoroughly enjoyed his holiday. Holidays for him were a time to relax and unwind for a few days and spend some precious time with his beautiful wife. He knew he was very lucky. He had sat oblivious to his surroundings, on the last day, on the beach, enjoying his book and watching her bob up and down in the sea. As he raised his eyes, looking out towards Penny, appearing and disappearing below the waves, he smiled and waved; he was sure he met her gaze, establishing that thread that joined them so closely together. John had watched the children playing around him and wondered what it would have been like to have a family like his brother. Rosie was a credit to them, bright, generous and loving. Sam was a delight, lively, amusing and entertaining everyone with his antics, but a few hours with them was enough! Playing 'uncle' was fun in bursts but he had never fancied himself as a dad, had never wanted that responsibility; he was not the 'father' type. Children often irritated or bored him – "No," he thought decisively, he would never have wanted or chosen his brother's path and life.

After almost twenty years of marriage, he knew Penny instinctively. He knew she was restless, that she needed friends, fun and freedom, and he was aware that he sometimes neglected her for his work – but that was their way – that was why they had never had children. They had been selfishly wrapped up in their own lives but unselfishly, too, wrapped up in each other. For a few weeks now, however, he had become concerned. She had become more inconsistent, one moment she was excitable, more demanding of his time and energy, particularly in the bedroom; his own memories locked in a smile of enticing amusement suddenly; the next moment she was quiet and distracted, reserved. Lately he was sensing a distance between them, working its way into their settled, contented lives. John picked up the plans and indulged himself with the hypnotic figures and measurements. He'd talk to Penny tonight, at the right moment. They'd readdress things and rebalance their lives in some honest talk, which was 'their way'. He suddenly remembered she was going out with Sue. They'd talk soon.

Penny and Sue always had a great night out, although Penny felt that Sue drank far too much. Although they danced and chatted comfortably like many old friends do, the last hour or so was always rather disappointing. Sue would be annoyingly loud and rude, having consumed so much alcohol, and she would end up being lumbered with some unpleasant, foul-breathing old man wanting to take her home. Despite this likely end, the dancing and energy of the clubs felt exhilarating and Penny loved it! Tonight was no exception, but as she sat sipping her Bacardi and Coke, waiting for Sue to return from the toilets, her mind settled on thoughts of Marjorie.

She had never really felt comfortable with her 'motherliness'. She had the impression Marjorie was dominated by her husband and children. Lately, though, she had developed an interest in this new, independent Marjorie, who had begun studying A Levels with an ambition to teach and establish a career. Recently, she had found her quite animated and interesting, and they were beginning to establish a genuine friendship. They began to spend more time chatting over tea and occasionally a glass of wine during the weekends. Rosie, too, would often join them; she was so grown up. When Marjorie started her second year and was preparing for the ultimate examinations, Penny, attracted by her sister-in-law's inner strength, was drawn to this liberated woman. She was also quietly surprised by Jim. He was obviously much more open-minded than she had judged him to be; he was quite a modern man and she found it quite attractive. Penny was aware that her opinions these days were becoming quite flirtatious and unnecessarily pompous – not all men were Neanderthals!

Marjorie continued to impress Penny, now with her dyed hair and short bob. She was looking much younger, she thought. The skirt she wore last week at dinner was not her usual style. The pleated insert was very becoming. It crossed her mind momentarily that she might be jealous. She smiled inwardly at her own rather condescending attitude and somewhat emulous observations. She decided that she now liked Marjorie a lot and wanted to involve her much more in her own life. She'd always liked Rosie of course, subtly independent and wise; now she was also captivated by her mother. She was going to ask Marjorie to go clubbing with her and Sue – soon – after her examinations of course: she would be too busy studying until then.

John and Jim had never really been very alike, but they were brothers. As John glanced round lightly, taking in the surroundings of the sparse living area, the heavy curtains, and oak furniture producing dark shadows across the walls and deep pile carpet, he was reminded of the time he and Jim had played hide-and-seek at their grandparents'. He was young, about five or six, and enthralled by the anticipation of being found. He could recall quite vividly watching Jim deftly explore the possibilities of concealment in the room and contemplating venturing further afield. Once out of sight, John sat quietly and started browsing the latest comic the paper boy had delivered, while his younger brother called out, "I'm ready!" Finally he loped towards his hiding place with false surprise, nonchalant and uninspired by his brother's love for fun and games. Similarly a memory of Jim splashing around in the sea usurped his memories, probably motivated by the recent holiday. They had been on a beach somewhere on the south coast. Jim had called to him to come and play, jumping the waves with a child's boundless energy, but he was happy on his own building a small, tower-like sandcastle for the tiny crabs he had found in a rock pool, further along the beach, away from everyone, enjoying his own company, engrossed in the sheltered sea world. He did of course venture several minutes later into the sea to join his brother, who was genuinely fun to be around, but he had realised about that time that they were very different, bound by the bonds of brotherhood, rather than any instinctive desire for friendship. Penny, he felt, was the same with her family. She was an only child, but her cousins, aunts and uncles had always been close. She had remained independent from them – though, he reflected, Penny had a similar lust for life, like Jim. Perhaps, he considered, he had been a bit boring!

It was a Thursday evening when Penny and Sue arrived to pick up Marjorie in a taxi. She was oozing excitement, dressed in a new pale blue top and black trousers. The black shoes, with a modest heel, added to the youthful look. She had passed her A Levels, achieving a 'B' for her English A Level, and a 'C' for Art. Although she had only managed a 'D' for Geography, she had really enjoyed studying the course and knew that her daughter had helped her make the right choice, and now she was enrolled at the local higher education college to study for a degree in Education. She couldn't be happier. She had worried that her newfound independence would bother Jim and the children, but it was the opposite: while she was happy and out and about, they could relax and engage in their own pastimes, dissolve into their own worlds of friends and places, without any interference.

The three 'girls' arrived outside the 'Lion and Lamb' pub, just a few yards from the club. It was busy with mostly younger drinkers, although there was always quite an eclectic mix, which made it a friendlier place to begin the evening's frivolities. Marjorie loved people-watching. She noticed a rather good-looking man standing and talking to a couple of girls, probably in their early twenties, and envied their confidence. He was with someone she thought she recognised, but it was hard to tell from the back of his head and across the crowded room. Everyone seemed to have a charming, light-hearted confidence about them – even the more mature occupants of this animated space.

Sue dived in first, with a round of two Bacardi and Cokes and a vodka and lime for Penny. There was no room to sit down, so they rested their drinks on a shelf next to a large rubber plant, tucked their bags between their feet and shouted their way through stories of the latest events in their lives, looking spasmodically towards the bar and across the room at the other people enjoying themselves.

"He's nice." Sue nodded towards a group of young men enjoying a private joke, at a table next to the door. The blond-haired youth was probably half their age but the pleasure was in the looking, not the action – rather like looking at a huge diamond on a ring, in a jewellery shop window, beautiful to admire and drool over, not something you would indulge in and buy, far too expensive and out of your reach...even for Penny...maybe. She had a tempting twinkle, not unnoticed by Sue and Marjorie.

"He's far too young for you," Sue remarked spontaneously.

"No harm in looking. Besides, I'd kill him!" she laughed with a suggestive, wild abandonment that slightly shocked but amused Marjorie.

She enjoyed their company, their energy, although like anything rich and exciting, going out with them and tasting such opulent pleasures was exhausting and not to be nourished too often. She was enjoying their interest in her studies and future plans and she was warming to Penny, whom she had thought of as rather aloof and unkind on occasion: "A self-satisfied prude," she had once said to Jim. She regretted the outburst now; it was ungracious. She knew she had made similar cutting comments about her in the past, not that Marjorie could remember them, small and insignificant observations that would be flatly denied now. She was becoming part of her new adventure: a career woman and wife, rather than a housebound mother and frump! Yes, she thought, she was very happy – and Jim was happy, too. Sex had become as adventurous and promising as her life. They'd become much more of a couple as they explored opportunities in the bedroom. Recently, now that the children were beginning to have their own lives, they had focused on their own relationship. A picture of Sam banging on the wall and telling them to stop making "silly noises" interrupted her musing and made her smile.

The queue to the club was extending out towards the car park. The lasers could be seen lighting up the sky, flickering rays of blues and greens, shooting straight lines of energy, transforming the black backdrop and throbbing to the beat, calling eager clubbers, like church bells to the congregation, but with a powerful and demanding energy.

They entered through the heavy doors onto the black and red, thick swirling patterns of the indulgent carpet, leading them and the other visitors past the booth, where their hands were stamped with a red blurred logo, an indistinctive pattern that would last for a couple of days. Working their way round the black and mirrored walls into the lounge bar, they found a place to sit along one side, facing small tables and welcoming armchairs and sofas. The high stalls and tables perched round the dance floor were filling up, too, lit up like a kaleidoscope by the video screen and lights. Soon they would be joining the writhing bodies of the dance crowd, strobed in strange electric rhythms.

Just now, the three women sat watching and drinking. Penny and Sue were smoking and singing at intervals to music that suddenly connected them to a time or place. Marjorie did not smoke because it made her cough, but the lyrics of the songs which linked her to her own youthful days were like an irresistible drug, and she belted out the few memorable lines she could remember and took another sip of her drink. Marjorie would soon be up on the dance floor, whether there were others dancing or not. She loved dancing. She had forgotten how much until now. Penny would be joining her soon, Sue more reluctantly. This was something Penny and she had in common. Penny was dancing her way through life without a care in the world.

Over the regular loud beat of the music, just loud enough to be heard, Penny suddenly blurted out, "I'm having an affair!" Sue and Marjorie's shocked faces were instinctive, amusing Penny for a moment. The alcohol had helped her speak out, confidently, but now she was a little ashamed of this brazen outburst.

"It just happened," she added, almost as an excuse. Well, that wasn't quite true: she had been attracted to Geoff for a while. She'd found herself flirting with him in John's office a couple of times and he was a renowned bachelor – there was never going to be any complicated relationship with him – just sex.

Marjorie immediately thought of John, Jim's brother, the family, how could she? But she knew she could, because it was Penny. She felt a lack of surprise, after the initial confidence had been divulged so openly. But she also felt a sadness creeping over her, a sense of loss.

"What about John?" Marjorie couldn't help herself.

"Oh, he knows – I think – we've talked. He wants me to get it out of my system." Sue was intrigued. They had made their way back to a space on a nearby sofa and she was now leaning forward in anticipation, like it was some sort of soap opera episode. Marjorie's mood had quietened, she'd lost her energy and life had slowed down under a heavy blanket. She knew how lucky she was with her family, her marriage and children. She would never contemplate indulging in a random affair, even if she was unhappy – it would not be worth it – it wasn't right! She got up with a finality, decisive and slightly dismissive, stating, "I'm off to dance," leaving the two of them to discuss the intricacies of the situation.

Marjorie enjoyed flirting with the men and dancing with abandonment, releasing her restless inner self. She was trying to shake off the rather sombre mood placating the scene since Penny's abrupt confession. It was working. The disco beat, with the rhythmic lights, absorbed her senses and brought her back to life. The tall, good-looking man opposite her encouraged her performance with his own sensuous and agile moves. Flirting was fun, but there would never be anyone else for her – only Jim.

CHAPTER 12

Rosie was packing her bag for school as her mother looked wistfully at the dishes in the sink, attempting to clean up after breakfast. Marjorie had ten full weeks stretching out in front of her, having completed the second year of her degree in education. Rosie continued to enjoy secondary school and with just one more week to go before the end of her fourth year, she was feeling relaxed and satisfied. Marjorie, although distracted by her thoughts, looked admiringly at the lovely young woman Rosie had become.

Rosie glanced up. "It's okay, Mum, Auntie Penny just needs some space. Uncle John will wait." Her mother was not surprised by her words of reassurance. Although she had not mentioned anything to anyone, she walked towards her, gave her a gentle kiss on the head and then hugged her. "Thank you." Words were often succinct. They understood each other, always had done and unnecessary conversation was often wasted. Marjorie was aware at that moment that Rosie was unusually quiet and sensitive herself.

"Is something troubling you?"

"I think I'm losing it…the gift."

"But you just said…"

"I know…I feel and sort of know things still, but I don't see it like I used to. I think I'm changing."

"We'll you're growing up," was her mother's obvious and natural reply. "No one can stop growing up and changing – not even you," she continued.

"Yes, I see, but it makes me feel sad and a bit worried – a bit worried about Sam…"

"Sam! – what's wrong with Sam?" her mother interjected.

"Nothing, I don't think so anyway…It's just a nagging," Rosie added. Both of them were aware that he was drawn to some rather unsavoury locals and had been caught smoking weed in the park by the local policeman, and, although Marjorie was convinced that their loving family love would see him through this difficult time in his life, Rosie wasn't so sure.

Rosie loved the way her mother spoke openly and with such honesty. Studying had given her a more interesting, admirable quality that they were all enjoying. The brief conversations they had now were regular, always purposeful, and they were more like friends than mother and daughter recently.

When her Auntie Penny invited her around for tea, she was not surprised. Her mother had some reading to do in preparation for the beginning of term. Her dad was going to tackle the garden – again: the lawn was looking neglected, and Sam was out with his friends – somewhere. He never left a note, just went wandering off and when he was grounded, just slipped out when no one was looking. It was difficult to discipline him as he took punishment lightly and there was a fear that if pushed too hard, he would run off somewhere. Although as a family they were very concerned, there was also an unmentioned confidence, that if something bad was to happen, Rosie would know about it and would know what to do.

She had packed a small bag with her brush, purse, a book and a bottle of water. She also packed her nightie and toothbrush – just in case – leaving a note on the kitchen table, so as not to disturb her mother. She spoke to her dad about her plans on the way out, as he stopped to rake up the mown grass. She often caught the bus and the journey was easy enough. The walk down the footpath, through the park to the bus stop, brought back a few childhood memories: hiding in the trees, making dens and swinging endlessly on the now rusting poles of the aged swing, now facing a bald patch, which once housed the Witches Hat. What a great time they had on that, a great climbing frame that swung round and from side to side, as they hung on, standing or sitting on the metal bars. They would spend hours challenging its aerodynamics with their human forces, as various children pushed and pulled, moving it violently high. Children either loved it or avoided it, but missed it terribly when the council removed it, considering it too dangerous, adding to their demise across the parks of England.

The park was a place of freedom, of childhood. Her friends met there several times during the week, after school, chatting, reading comics as they sat about on the grass or benches or on the roundabout. They would swing effortlessly or join a long line at the top of the slide, before travelling in a tightly held group, slowly and awkwardly to the bottom, in a train. Those days would drift away like their friendships, as they grew older and more independent, and moved on. As she approached her sixteenth birthday, Rosie began to long for those days in the park and her youth. She was involved with the relationships of friends and their boyfriends. Her own few dates with Colin were uneventful and fraught with misunderstandings. Apart from holding hands, sitting together and enjoying conversations and the company of their group of friends, the occasional non-committal kiss and a visit to the cinema, it was a generally unremarkable time. She was conscious of the fact that she spent much less time at home and with her parents, who seemed quite happy with their own company. Sam would be in the third year of secondary school after the holidays. He had settled in well, confidently and enthusiastically. He was doing well. The demise of her feelings and visions was an obvious reflection of her own involvement in life: she was too busy to think, and she was less appreciative of any voices or concerns that might try to haunt her.

Rosie arrived at her Auntie Penny's shortly after six o'clock on the Friday; her satchel hung heavily over her shoulder, bulging with encumbering textbooks and exercise books displaying half a term's thoughtful work in neat, legible handwriting. Her high grades completed each page, inadvertently summing up the teachers' encouraging comments, splattered in red ink. She was welcomed enthusiastically by her aunt as the door opened, defusing the tense air that had been lingering inside. John was upstairs somewhere, the effusive tinkling of strings from his guitar filtering down; evidence of his presence. She followed Penny automatically into the kitchen, where she was in the act of preparing a simple tea of cheese on toast. The oily, bubbling mass was dribbling over the edges of the toast, browning under the grill.

"Orange juice? Squash? Tea?" her questions inviting a response of confirmation.

"Just water, please…Have you got any Ribena?"

"Oh, yes, somewhere…" Penny began rummaging effortlessly in the cupboard, finding an out-of-date darkening liquid.

"Just water will be fine," she offered with a grin, both laughing at her aunt's lack of domesticity.

The easy mood opened up the pending conversation, like rolling out the red carpet to invite importance. Penny's thoughts stepped onto it cautiously.

"I'm not sure what I should do, Rosie. He's had a few

girlfriends, you know."

"Well, you've had boyfriends, Auntie," confirming the situation. "Don't you think it's a waste?"

"Do you?"

For the first time Rosie felt irritated. Why did everything always have to come down to what she thought and felt? Why couldn't people just get on with their own lives? She had become bored with following her incessant instincts and giving advice; their "perfect treasure" she knew was becoming a rather aggrieved teenager. This sudden outburst of thoughts was quite new to her and she knew that growing up was going to be a challenge she hadn't contemplated before.

Rosie sighed conclusively. Penny reacted immediately. She was sensitive to her niece's obvious irritation. Despite not having children of her own, she was close to her and yet separate enough to sense things perhaps her parents overlooked.

"Are you okay, Roz?" The nickname was intimately theirs and it engaged Rosie's warmth and friendship again.

"I'm just being a teenager!" Exasperation evident in the release of this exclamation. "And – I'm losing my gift, Auntie," she concluded with finality.

Penny reached over thoughtfully and held her hand lightly. "Maybe it's a good thing – and maybe I should be making my own mind up? I would genuinely like to know what you think, though," she added.

"I know." Realising the irony behind these words, they laughed again.

John ventured into the kitchen as they were munching their way through their toast, Penny sipping a glass of wine, Rosie finishing her iced water.

"Hi!" He bent over and gave Rosie a welcoming peck on the cheek, looking up towards his wife, comfortable in their presence, despite the obvious interruption. He grabbed a couple of biscuits from the cupboard and put the kettle on. Rosie was amused by this, reflecting on her own parents in the kitchen; her father a stranger to the workings of kitchen technology and a cupboard's hidden treasures; their kitchen surfaces cluttered with letters, books and other abandoned debris, as the family entered through the back door and passed through, depositing unwanted items at the first available opportunity. The draining board was littered with plates, pans and mugs, despite her mother's constant attempts to keep up with the washing and cleaning as well as working. Her mother had pottered around tirelessly and relentlessly, following her family around in an endless whirl of housework; the house was managed systematically in a previous life. Now she was teaching, the house was a jumble.

Sam only visited the kitchen when there was food to be had or a distinct possibility of refreshment from the fridge. Rosie wandered in and out, whenever she felt some help was needed, offering her services with the ease and support of a well-loved relative – just like her grandmother, she mused and thoughts of her grandmother, Sylvia, rested for a moment until she returned to the more clinical, kempt kitchen of her aunt and uncle's home. In the short silence that ensued, a gentle comfort layered the table, like a cloth preparing for the clatter of plates.

"Do you want me to get you anything?"

"No, Penny, I'm fine. Do you both want a Chinese later?" Rosie had picked at the toast with burnt edges and crusting cheese, trailing a pool of oil on the plate. She looked up at her aunt, smiled and nodded. Penny's more languid nod followed.

"That would be lovely."

The new Chinese Emporium had opened last year and was a favourite haunt of theirs. Rosie's first taste of sweet and sour was not a particularly pleasant one – too sickly and the batter too stodgy, but she had had mushrooms in black bean sauce and a pancake roll since and she had enjoyed the light, crispy batter and crunchiness, dipped in the flavours of soya sauce. She had suggested a Chinese to her parents once, but her father was happier with fish and chips or a home-cooked meal, although there were fewer of them these days and Vesta curries had crept into their weekly menu. Her mother dutifully accepted his viewpoint – until recently. Rosie and her mum had arranged to go to the newly opened Indian Spice House with her Auntie

Penny, only last week. Foreign food was becoming popular across the country, although mainly young couples were indulging in the experience and expense.

When John had left the kitchen, Rosie and Penny resumed their conversation, Penny starting up with a decisive statement.

"I've decided to stay, refocus on my marriage – on John. He really has become quite 'modern', you know. He even came with me to a club last Saturday." Rosie laughed at the vision that caught her imagination, of Uncle John knocking out moves on the dance floor, in an open-necked shirt and jeans. Penny understood her look of amusement. "He doesn't dance...well, not until he has had a few pints of beer and then everyone is drunk enough not to care." They were laughing again, like old friends rather than an aunt and her niece, Penny sensing Rosie's unmentioned happiness at her decision, simply stated:

"You're right! Maybe it is better to make our own decisions. We've all relied on you far too much": a conclusive ending to their idle chatter. She got up, refilled their glasses and ventured into the living room, followed closely by her niece, to watch the television. John was already settled, watching a favourite sitcom.

CHAPTER 13

It seems life has a way of undulating in a flux of insecure melodramas. As soon as the journey is stable, running smoothly, happiness steadying the rocking boat, an incident either shatters the calm like a freak storm, or ripples until huge waves engulf everyone, drowning them in sadness. Not long after Rosie had visited her aunt and uncle's, she felt the familiar anxiety caused by a knowledge that something bad was going to happen; only lately she was unable to detect what that 'thing' would be. There would be no warning, no helpful advice, except an uncontrollable need to be vigilant. It was late on a Sunday afternoon in June, when her periods finally arrived, like an unwelcome visitor. She had expected the intrusion into her life for a while but its arrival was still a surprise – and concern. She felt a sense of loss immediately. It felt like an evil blackness had crept in and held her down and she was convinced this was the catalyst for her lack of 'sight'.

As Penny and John settled back into a contented married life and Rosie's mum continued to follow her career, becoming more confident and more alive, engaging everyone around her, particularly her father, with an admirable vivacity that Rosie was keen to mimic, Rosie became less troubled by her turbulent teenage feelings and more settled, too. Even Sam was working on achieving success with his studies, and his regular stays at his grandmother's were enthusiastically welcomed, his well-developed friendship with Paul providing him with an energy and purpose that filtered through the school week. He never wanted to come home from London, preferring to be spoilt by his gran. Last weekend, as Jim cheerfully bounced in through the door, he was followed by a disgruntled Sam.

"But why can't I go and stay next weekend? Paul and I had something planned…"

"Come on, Sam, cheer up – it's only one weekend. Give your nan a break." Marjorie came out from the kitchen, wiping her wet hands on her skirt.

"How was she?"

"Brilliant!" he beamed. He had been concerned the last few visits. His mother seemed rather frail these days and he was convinced she was not eating properly. She seemed to have shrunk into herself and the sparkle in her eyes had faded. He knew how much she missed Stanley, but she still refused to move nearer to Jim and the family; she had even used the excuse that Sam would not be able to play with Paul, now referred to as his "best buddy". But today was different. She had been pruning in the garden, baked a cake for his arrival, and she had her sparkle back – he was convinced there was someone lighting that torch, igniting her hidden flame. She had not offered to invite Sam for the next weekend. She had other plans, it seemed.

When the telephone rang, late on Wednesday afternoon, nearly two weeks later, Rosie was aware of a helplessness and concern for her father – and for Sam. She suddenly felt nervous. She hovered over the telephone as her mother went to pick it up, softly laying her hand on her mother's, aware that her senses were suddenly heightened. Rosie's look of concern was enough for Marjorie to take a short breath and prepare herself for whatever, whoever, was bringing bad news – news she knew she did not want to hear. Sylvia had fallen. She was in hospital. She had a fractured pelvis and several bruises and cuts – she was stable. Marjorie let out a breathless sigh, unaware that she had been holding her breath, as the last three words delivered the relief she so badly sought.

The journey to the hospital reminded them of that other time – the visit to see Grandad Stanley; a last visit and an untimely death. This journey reeked of a similar ominous odour. Sam chatted about how fit Grandma was and how he could look after her when he visited next weekend. He could make her meals and shop and tidy and… his lively, excitable talk full of nervous energy – a nervousness everyone recognised. Rosie began to feel guilty. She knew what her parents would be thinking – "wasn't there some sign – some warning?"

"Will she be alright?" her father asked hopefully and Rosie's nonchalant shrug and silent tears just confirmed what they had already come to realise: she had lost her 'sight', and the sense of loss penetrated the family with a sadness and reluctant melancholy.

Unlike their visit to see Stanley, however, they were welcomed by a smiling Sylvia.

Although she was fashioning some large, purple bruises and was plastered heavily, unable to manoeuvre herself, she looked positively well. Sam rushed up to her bedside and laid his head on her shoulder, kissing her healthier cheek gently. Realising abruptly that his rather zealous behaviour was rather childish at twelve years old, he stood up and grinned.

"Hi, Gran. You okay?"

"I'm fine." Sylvia looked around at her dear family and their anxious faces and felt emotions welling up, stifling sobs of helplessness and allowing the horrific fear of death she had felt to be released inexorably. Gathering her demeanour, she smiled at Rosie in a light-hearted gesture:

"I wish you could have warned me, Rosie, not to rush out to the washing when it was raining! I slipped badly. I've never known the path to be that slippery when wet!"

She winked warmly and the family settled comfortably

into idle chatter about the accident, her recovery and speculating how long it would be before she came home. Sylvia's comments about the handsome doctor assured them all that she was very much fit of mind, if not of body. They left a much happier group than the one that had arrived.

"See you, Gran," Sam chirped.

The pain seeped through her body as she physically relaxed after they had gone. The excruciating pain that had been numbed by the painkillers administered a couple of hours before was wearing off. She rang the alarm and lay back uncomfortably into the starched pillow. By the time the nurse came with medicine to help relieve her suffering, Sylvia was feeling decidedly unhappier. This was going to be a hard battle to win.

The doctor had implied that it would take several weeks, maybe a couple of months, before she could return home and then she would need a lot of support. The severity of the break meant she might not be able to walk far on her own. When it became evident that she was not healing as well as they had hoped, it was decided that Jim and Marjorie would collect her and a bed would be put up temporarily in the dining room, while she was 'on the mend'.

Loss of privacy was the immediate problem for Rosie and Marjorie. Rosie used the dining room to study, Marjorie to mark. Sam was missing his friend Paul, now that he could not stay in London, and Jim started staying later at work to 'get things done'. It was difficult. Sylvia was becoming cantankerous because she wanted her own space, too; her home; her independence. Life was becoming strangled and sensitive. As Marjorie made yet another cup of tea in the kitchen, Rosie attempted to ease the situation.

"Why don't you and I go round to Auntie Penny's, when Dad gets home?"

"Is that what you think we should do?" She could not help herself. Rosie had always made suggestions that worked out to be just what was right or needed.

"I'm sorry, Mum...I don't know...but you know we both could do with a bit of a break from Gran, even if we love her dearly."

"What about your dad?"

"To be honest, Mum, he's not here all day!" There was annoyance in her tone, that she had been unable to disguise. Her mother had been given time off work to tend to her mother-in-law, until after half-term and Rosie's studies were suffering. Sam was often in his bedroom these days, playing Subbuteo or off on his bike. He had become more dependent on his local mates, Steven and Lewis, now that there was an impossible distance between him and Paul. He'd roll in about nine o'clock, grab some toast, loaded with brown sugar or treacle, and retire to his bedroom and eventually to bed. He loved his grandmother, but she was too frail to be fun and all she did was moan all the time.

He was grieving for the grandmother of last year, for his weekends with Paul. Lewis and Steven were an outlet for his independence. It was also different now and he missed his visits to his grandparents' house. He suddenly felt nostalgic. The family were suffering. Jim and Marjorie's relationship was becoming strained, too. A sense of loss and longing for the past consumed them.

Normality and structure had dissipated. In their place a strange, day-by-day programme evolved around Grandma Sylvia's needs and the family's attempts at a stable, working environment. Sylvia was walking tentatively now and managing a few simple chores, the abundance of cups of tea an indication of her newfound self-sufficiency. But she was frail and her lust for life diminished to "a stumbling old fossil", words she had mustered from her thoughts of Stanley, words he would have used about her in a loving, affable way. Marjorie had returned to work and except for a nurse who popped in at least three times a week, Sylvia was the loneliest she had ever been.

Penny, Marjorie and Rosie worked their way through a packet of chocolate digestives, tea and a couple of glasses of wine and a bottle of Cherryade for Rosie. Their visits to Penny's were a weekly Wednesday treat for Rosie and her mother. It was relaxing and fun. Often when they arrived, Penny would open the door promptly, eager and waiting. She would hustle them quickly into the neat dining room, rarely used and with an untouched model magazine appearance, both beautiful and stark. On the table were cakes and sandwiches, obviously not of her making, without the care and abundance of a mother's love in the kitchen, but neat and exact, bought as delicacies from the expensive bakery idolised by the wealthy. She enjoyed these family get-togethers, absorbed by their chatter, despite the depressing subjects they tended to discuss. There was a light-hearted appeal in the women's group. She missed some of the friends she'd neglected as she had indulged herself in John's attention and focused on their marriage. Sue was one of those who had abandoned her. She wanted to party and did not like it when Penny preferred to spend a night out with her husband instead of her. The talk that evening was all about Sylvia. There did not seem to be an obvious solution, but the family was hurting. Rosie had no solution either.

When Marjorie and Rosie returned home that evening, Sylvia was in tears, and Jim had gone out and Sam was hidden away upstairs in his room, leaving her alone again. Perched on her makeshift bed, Sylvia looked away from them and wept softly.

"I want to go home. I miss home… I miss Stanley." Her grief consumed the room.

"Oh Mum." Marjorie didn't know what to say. Rosie moved towards her and sat gently next to her on the bed, the hardness disguised by her grandmother's thick eiderdown.

"It's okay to be sad, Grandma, but we want to look after you."

"I'm a nuisance; I'm in the way and Jim needs his home and family back."

Neither of them could really argue with these obvious observations; they had been discussing precisely those sentiments with Penny.

"But Mum, you're not well enough. You haven't been eating and drinking properly for the last couple of weeks and we're worried about you."

Her words of comfort and concern were genuine, but it was evident that Marjorie was hoping for some sort of solution to what had become a constant source of anxiety. Aware of Rosie's helpful presence, she moved to leave them.

"I'll go and look for Jim." Marjorie excused herself and left them to talk. Rosie looked up and smiled, confirming her decision. She was feeling more at ease with herself in this moment of crisis and gave herself up to the words and feelings that were nagging at her at that moment.

"I know you miss Grandad, Stanley – terribly," she added, sensing the intensity of the old woman's grief, "but think of all the wonderful things to come, holidays, weddings, great-grandchildren one day." She grinned. "There's so much for you still to do and life to live..." she tapered off, sensing such a useless list of delights was not penetrating this dear lady's thoughts. "It will get better," she promised, but she was feeling the complete opposite to be true. Sylvia had, she knew, picked up on it all.

"You are a wonderful, beautiful granddaughter," her sincerity lingering, "but these dreams, these 'visions' are yours – you have a wonderful life ahead of you, but mine – well, it's ambling along, painfully, and I don't want to go on without Stanley," she admitted, judging her honesty to be safe with her granddaughter. They hugged, a generous, decisive hug, completed with a warm and knowing look, ending the matter and concluding what they both acknowledged as a heartfelt, loving, farewell moment.

Rosie was as cheery as she could be the following morning, when she suggested that Grandma move home. It wasn't a decision they would take lightly but Jim recognised a renewed determination to his mother's request, reminding him of his daughter's words a few years before: "It was his time." A great sadness engulfed him as he helped her pack up and settled her back home to the place she belonged.

It was a rather chilly October evening when Jim settled his mum in for the night, kissing her forehead softly. She was definitely more at ease in her own home, and as normality was regained in his own home, he felt the anxiety of the last few months slipping away. He knew his mother had been enjoying the company of her neighbours and she was moving more, less dependent on her walking frame and eating more heartily. He was convinced now that moving her back home had been the right thing to do. Turning to leave, he suddenly noticed that the beautiful vase that had pride of place on the mantelpiece had vacated its prize spot.

"Where's Grandma's vase, Mum?"

"Oh, you know, I'm not sure. I might still have it packed away in one of those boxes," she suggested, rather confused and disorientated. Not wanting to pry, Jim accepted this and left, not totally convinced by her vagueness and slightly irritated, too, with his concern for a piece of china over his mother's well-being.

The irritation he felt over a few items going missing over the next couple of weeks grew. Sam, who had begun to visit regularly again, spending time with his gran, as well as with his friend Paul, had become more of a mentor, watching over his gran and making sure she locked the back door and closed windows. He answered the door keenly for her and reminded her not to let anyone in. He had become very protective, "her little soldier". On one visit, Sam went to the cupboard to lay out her best blue china for tea, as a special treat. He had brought some cream cakes round. Looking at the empty shelf, he called to her from the front room:

"Where's your best china, Gran?"

"Oh, don't worry, I have met a very nice man, an antique dealer, actually. He has taken it to have it valued. I don't really need it and I thought I'd give the money to your mum and dad – a sort of thank you for looking after me. Don't go telling them, I want it to be a surprise. He says it might be worth quite a lot of money." Sam was concerned that a strange man had wandered off with it, and even more unhappy about the fact she might sell it; he knew how fond of it his mother and particularly Rosie were, but she talked about her friend in such a convincing way, noticeably brightening up as she talked about him, that he decided not to say anything to upset her. The man she enthused about had been cleaning her windows and often popped in for a cup of tea and a chat. She described him as rather rugged-looking but with sexy eyes. He was quite young, it seemed, but very amusing and helpful.

To reassure himself, he asked his friend Paul to act as his private detective while he was home, keeping a vigilant eye on her and her property. The following week, as his dad left to visit, he confided in him about his concerns.

"You should have said something before." He spoke brusquely, his own concerns surfacing.

"Sorry, Dad, but she seems really happy."

"Okay. You've been brilliant," he began, composing himself and suddenly feeling rather embarrassed by his sudden sharpness. "Sorry I snapped. I'll have a chat with her."

Jim's concerns increased after his visit and he spoke to his mother about arranging for a locksmith to change the locks. He decided to ring the police on Monday, to inform them of his concerns, if the items hadn't been returned by then. It was Saturday and when he got in about teatime, he spoke to Marjorie about it.

"Oh, Jim, not the beautiful blue china tea set, and the ruby brooch?"

"He's promised to bring them back tomorrow with the valuations, so I will check on her tomorrow evening before I do anything rash."

"What does Rosie think?" Jim was not surprised by Marjorie's reliance on Rosie: she was usually sound in her views and decisions, although lately neither of them had bothered her. She seemed to be enjoying life and was less involved in her parents' activities and conversations. Just then, she walked in the room.

"I think you should call the police." Whether she had been listening at the door or just offering that instinctive and impulsive advice that she sometimes did, her parents acted immediately, and her father picked up the telephone. The police promised to visit her on Monday to take a statement. Jim would be there after work. There was an alarming tension filtering from the room when Sam walked in through the front door, discarding his boots momentously in the hallway, but he ignored it and bounded up the stairs avoiding the heaviness surrounding the three conspirators, in his usual search for a carefree life.

CHAPTER 14

Jim parked the car. It wasn't until he was near the front door that he noticed it was slightly ajar. He pushed it open cautiously and immediately noticed that the drawers of the dresser in the hall were open and papers and items were scattered on the floor.

"Sylvia." His voice sounded dry and cracked. The house had obviously been ransacked. The fright had been too much for her frail heart and Jim found his lovely mother dead, clutching onto a picture of the family: the one in the silver frame they had bought her for Christmas. The police were attentive and thorough. The limited information Sam had been able to provide was noted, but no one had seen anything, including Paul.

Grief consumed the whole family, but Sam's world had collapsed dramatically. He felt guilty as if he was somehow responsible for the care of his grandmother. He was angry with Paul for not having been there, for not noticing anything. His grief made him angry; his behaviour and personality became increasingly more thoughtless and selfish.

Rosie's senses had heightened considerably since her

grandmother's death. It was, she believed, as if, once her grandparents had been reunited in death, her powers had been restored. She had no control, however, over her visions and thoughts, they came and went unexpectantly and without warning. She was frustrated that she could not read her brother or know what he was up to. She worried about him constantly. She knew he was smoking pot and hanging out with Paul again in London, but when he disappeared, she was as surprised as her parents. Why hadn't she seen that coming?

It was a Thursday and he had emptied his schoolbag over the dining table, Marjorie instantly hoping he was about to settle to some homework, even though she was about to lay the table for tea. But grabbing his bag, he darted out of the back door. "I'm just going out to meet some friends!"

"What about your tea?" Marjorie shouted, her words left behind as he raced up the path. When he wasn't home by midnight, she telephoned the police, who recorded the details and said they would be round the following evening if he wasn't back by then, reassuring them that he would probably be back in a day or two and that it happened all the time. "Was he taking any drugs of any kind, did they know?" Of course the denial was not a confident one and didn't fool the police either.

"Don't you have any idea where he is, Rosie?"

"If I did, wouldn't I tell you?" Rosie felt her insides

screaming. This 'gift', as her grandfather had called it, was ripping her apart: years of access to it had moulded and shaken her long enough. It was useless when she most needed it and it interrupted her life when she longed for normality and peace. The violence of her frustrations triggered, she slung down the book she was attempting to lose herself in, while they waited for news, any news; while she waited for an inkling, any ideas, any sign to help find her troubled brother. How could he be so selfish? How could he cause his family so much heartbreak? She suddenly softened and moved to hug her mother. Both of them wept quietly: Marjorie for the son she felt she was losing, Rosie from exasperation.

They went to bed, to restless sleep. Marjorie was up and down the stairs, guiltily racking her brain for ideas of where he might be, of what he might be doing, pacing the living room with a nervous energy, twitching the curtains and gazing out into the night. They had tried his friends, rang Paul's aunt; there had been no answer and they had driven round aimlessly until they got too tired and too tearful to go on. They had gone to bed, hopeful that there would be good news in the morning, wanting daylight to come quickly, to rid them of the haunting blackness of the night that smothered them.

The next day, Marjorie and Jim went to work which kept their minds active and helped pass the time; Rosie also used the 'normality' of her studies to engage her thoughts, but the tight atmosphere at teatime was clouded by unspoken words and the imminent arrival of the local police who would be there soon to take a statement. Rosie could not help. She felt it like an abyss.

The second night, as they retired to bed, exhausted by grief and worry, they prepared themselves for another night of interrupted sleep. Rosie heard her mother get up. It must have been past midnight.

Marjorie felt better pacing, looking out of the window in hopeful expectation of his return. She finally crumbled onto the floor with exhaustion, clinging to the curtains which shielded the patio doors, waiting and waiting, sobbing weakly until she finally fell asleep about three o'clock in the morning. She was woken carefully by Jim as he left for work and ordered her to bed to rest. She dutifully did as she was told, like a small child. He rang work for her with some excuse of a virus. Rosie decided she could miss a lecture or two and sat upright in bed, half-listening to the voices and movements in the house and half-focusing on an essay on a case study she was working on. She loved studying Law, but at that moment it was more of a distraction to help her forget the turbulent worries that thundered in her head.

It was a strange day of phone calls, sympathies and concerns, as word filtered out that Sam had gone missing. Marjorie went back to work the next day, her wretched state confirming that she was definitely not well. Rosie tried to keep her focus on her studies while at the same time attempting to open up to her feelings, any clues she might have to his whereabouts. Jim was in an angry daze – what had he done wrong? What should he have done differently? Surely this was all his fault – or Marjorie's…their fault, the blame slightly shifting, to allow relief to his troubled brain.

It was two days later when Rosie got a call from an old school friend, someone she still saw around the village.

"I've seen him. He's at the Mobil garage with Paul and another older boy. They are sitting in a car. Hurry!"

She dived into her little Escort and made her way anxiously to find him, hoping he'd still be there but having no idea what she would say or do when she got there. She parked up in the first space available, jumped out and called over to him.

"Sam, get in this car now!" Her order was thick and controlled. He turned to say something to his companions and then climbed out of the small, black vehicle and made his way over towards her. There was a heaviness, a silence, as she drove him home. Outside their house, she reached over and grabbed his hand tightly as they walked up to the back door; the reassuring grip steadied her and connected them safely.

Sam wasn't concerned about his absence. He was rather enjoying the adventure. "I'm young but I can look after myself," he thought. Paul and his older mate, Terry, sat laughing on the sofa, idly watching a video. Sam knew he was pushing the barriers, but he wasn't doing any real harm… Although by the second evening he was considering whether perhaps some of the decisions he was making might be rather foolish. He hadn't given his family a thought until then. They were busy in their own worlds. He'd be in some trouble but that didn't concern him right now – or his friends. Terry had driven down from London with Paul especially, to catch up with Sam for a few days and have some fun. Paul's aunt was working a lot at the moment and had not worried about his 'extra guests'. The small spliff, shared, was part of the adventure, the excitement, the exploration of teenagers: there was no particular agenda or attempt to upset. Children need barriers; for Sam and his friends, these barriers had been left ajar and neglected through complacency. He knew his family were struggling to come to terms with his gran's death, but he didn't want to talk about it; he didn't want to be around their depressing moodiness, with their questioning looks and guilty remarks. None of that would bring her back. He felt a tug of sadness.

His sullen mood was suddenly lifted with the lively chatter of his friends. The boys sat idly, before wandering off to the corner shop for some cigarettes and sweets. Wandering the streets and hanging out was part of the adventure of growing up. There was always a comforting casualness about Paul that appealed to Sam. Suddenly his mate blurted out, "Who needs families!?" Paul himself was not quite sure what had initiated his outburst, but lately he had been dreaming of his mum – the mother who had abandoned him years ago, who had never got in touch and now had been bothering him in recurrent nightmares. His mates were more like a family and it was perhaps this sense of ease that enabled him to talk about her at last. Things unsaid, he knew, were causing his mind to create these nightly explosions of strange narratives and remind him of a mother long forgotten. Sam was first to offer a question of interest:

"What family? There's only your aunt."

"It's my mum. I haven't seen her for years and I keep wondering what happened to her. It's really stupid, because she left me and obviously doesn't think about what's happened to me." The boys were quiet, not sure whether to respond to Paul's spoken thoughts.

"Don't think about her, then. Let's go to the rec and kick a ball about," Terry offered, clearly and dismissively... and they did. Talk of family had disturbed Sam's thoughts momentarily, and, although he was temporarily disappointed when his sister collected him the following afternoon at the petrol station, he was almost relieved with the inevitable conclusion and his sister's conclusive rescue.

When Rosie rang her parents there was only relief. Instead of recriminations and restrictions, there were hugs and grateful silences. But there had been a change. Sam was more settled for a while. He'd had enough of adventure recently and was living off his exploits with his mates at school and trying to catch up, with limited success, the work he'd missed. He was missing his gran more deeply and went out and about more as a distraction, breathing life into any depressed states that nagged at him and keeping a distance from his sister. He was convinced she'd known all along where he was and what he was doing; it was uncomfortable – weird.

His mother walked on eggshells a bit in case he might run off again and his father asked him lots of questions; "Where are you going? What time are you back? Who are you with?" Sam didn't mind the attention, he quite liked it. It didn't bother him too much. He could still hang out with his mates, although Paul and his mate Terry were out of bounds. When they turned up at school and he wagged a couple of lessons or went offsite at lunchtime, no one seemed to notice or bother to report him. There was the truancy letter, but he winged the conversations with his parents and teachers, playing on their sympathies to his troubled state of mind and his promise to work harder and be better. Life resumed a normality, occasionally tinged with concern but settled in appearance.

The family had regained some stability and contentment

again, their lives running smoothly, but they were like visitors to a gallery, sharing observations and talking with some interest on occasion, but coming and going separately. Their mother and father were often ensconced on the sofa, watching television and eating bonbons or Liquorice Allsorts. Rosie would be chatting to friends on the telephone in the hall, and Sam would be off somewhere at a mate's, if they hadn't taken up residence in their individual bedrooms. The family would come together randomly in the kitchen or lounge intermittently and they would resume moments of intimacy.

A distance had grown between Rosie and her brother. He shied away from his all-knowing sister and she was irritated by his thoughtless independence. But today she needed him. He'd been back about an hour and was in his room. It was just after six o'clock and he was hungry. Her mum was cooking his favourite, ham, egg and chips – an easy, quick meal for a Monday, having just got in herself from work. Rosie was aware of her heightened senses since her grandmother had died, but she had been too busy to concern herself with such stimuli and nagging thoughts... That was until now. She had been completing a final dissertation when her head seemed to explode. A searing pain violently followed behind her eyes and then went just as sudden. The image she saw was clear: a woman's dead body.

Rosie stood quietly outside her brother's room. The door was firmly closed and she could hear his music thumping rhythmically in the background. She hesitated for a moment and then tapped on the door with a sense of urgency.

"Who is it?" He knew, but this was his room and he was reluctant to have his space invaded by his sister – or anyone at that moment. He was enjoying the light humour of some old comics he'd found under his bed. Rosie was not going to play his games and walked in, pausing slightly as she passed over the threshold.

"I need your help." Sam was immediately taken aback, looking cautiously at his sister. He hadn't really noticed how much she'd grown lately. Now, framed in the doorway, it was as if he was looking at her for the first time in years. Her long, brown hair was hanging gently over her shoulders, clipped helpfully on one side. Her eyes were dark, solid and forgiving. He supposed at that moment that he really loved his sister, but he'd grown up, too, and was much less welcoming of her charms.

"What can I help YOU with?" defining the 'you' with some animosity. He wasn't quite sure why he felt so antagonistic, but his irritation gripped him and held on with a determined force.

"There's been a murder and my senses have heightened. Dad's in trouble, so is Mum, and I need you to help me." It wasn't just this dramatic outburst that suddenly frightened him, but she seemed to crumble as the tears came and rushed over to the bed and hugged him impulsively. Sam immediately softened and allowed his arm to reach out and comfort his sister who seemed to have shrunk, all his emotions swirling in a confused mass, and he tried to make some sense of what had just happened, the word 'murder' lingering and pulsating in his head.

"I know Paul is involved," she blurted out, "but I don't know how and I need you to help me find out what's been going on or Dad will go to prison – I just know it – I've felt it – I've seen it," she continued in a further flurry of attempted explanation. This strange dramatic and effusive ranting was completely out of character. Rosie, always so composed and gentle with her hindsight, was gushing uncontrollably, like an efficacious script for a television crime drama. Just then the telephone rang from downstairs.

"It's Paul!" Mum yelled upstairs to Sam. Rosie and Sam looked at each other and alarm embraced them as they moved apart in response to her words.

"Tell him I'll ring him back shortly!" he shouted back and turned back to his sister.

"He says it's urgent!" his mother persisted.

"Go and see what he wants. We can talk after," Rosie offered. And her brother left the room.

CHAPTER 15

It was on a particularly warm June afternoon, a Wednesday at about two o'clock, when most people were at work, when the body was found. The police had set up a crime site in Rosemary and Allen's grounds, digging up her beautifully established plants and driving mud and grime across the elegant marble pool surround. Dirt found its way into the pool, the crisp, blue glow turning overnight into a murky pond. Rosemary was devastated. As well as the loss of income, while the Tuscan home was invaded by investigators, her home had become a place of intrigue and suspicion. It was going to be difficult to recover from this. Of course they felt sorry for the poor woman, so decomposed that it was difficult to identify the corpse, but this gory interruption to their lives couldn't have come at a worse time. They had been fully booked for the summer and just updated the gardens in preparation for their busiest time of the year.

Allen's financial budgeting and organisation would see them through this difficult time, but he was well aware that he lacked the empathy to share his wife's grief and loss. Her love for this place was deep, like a mother's love for a child. Their only child had been a victim of a cot death, and the energy and passion she had given to this project, their business and home, had helped her come to terms with her grief. The police had promised to return the property to its original state, but she was well aware that would take time and they would not be too concerned about the quality of the work. Rosemary was suddenly conscious of her heartless response to the crime scene and felt a sense of guilt, but she had always been self-sufficient and determined, and this had nothing to do with them. She was angry, concerned and seeing all their work being destroyed around them was affecting her judgement of the situation. "Why here? How on earth had the body got there in their garden?" Questions that hacked at her reasoning.

The phone rang amongst the pile of papers on Detective Inspector Ian Graham's desk. The body discovered in the small Tuscan village had caused great interest in Italy, but was of little importance to the British people, concerned only with their own tragedies and crimes. Forensics had already uncovered evidence to suggest this was a murder case: strangulation and possible rape. The body belonged to a Lucy Jameson, a British woman. Steven tried to establish the main facts, talking to someone from the local Italian Police, who spoke broken English in an incomprehensible fashion.

"She had marks round neck, maybe strangled – woman

about twenty or 30 – long time ago – ten year perhaps. Garden flood in rains and then body come up and dog find. We need you to come as is a British lady."

Although the thought of a trip abroad, to sunny Italy even better, appealed, the prospect of struggling to understand the lingo bothered him. Building up a picture and solving a case from simple monosyllabic statements was not his idea of fun! He knew Gina would be quite capable of helping him; an enthusiastic, intelligent officer, who had climbed the ladder as far as she could, due to her dark, foreign appearance and Italian parentage – she was a woman, too, and that didn't help. Ian liked her, though, despite the fact she was a woman and a foreigner. She had dealt well with the incessant bullying and comments. There was still a fair amount of prejudice in the force, but he could do nothing about that, but he could offer her this opportunity. Glancing through the vertical blinds, he could detect her form, waiting patiently outside his office, summoned by him in a moment of inspiration. He tapped on the window and beckoned her in.

"Please sit down, Gina." He spoke in a warm, engaging manner.

"Thank you." Her voice was soft but firm and, although the accent was defined, her diction was clear and audible.

"I need you to help me with a murder case in Italy." Her eyes brightened with interest.

"I need you to help me communicate with the local

police. I can't speak a word of Italian, a little French from my schooldays, but that's it...and I need someone I can trust." The obvious compliment was enough to engage her, but the idea of a murder case was even more appealing. She smiled confidently in response to the inspector's request, trying to subdue her excitement.

"I'd love that," she said simply. Her uses in the station were tedious and minimal. She knew so much more than many of the officers she worked with, but kept most of her ideas and thoughts to herself for fear of alienating herself more. Occasionally she would offer a suggestion on a case, which would be considered with some surprise and then acknowledged as the brainstorm of another white, male officer in the vicinity aiming to make his mark. Gina was used to this and accepting of her situation. She could not fight the system on her own and she was on her own: only one other policewoman worked on that floor in the station, all the other women were secretaries or cleaners. The conversation with Detective Inspector Graham was promising for her: a reward, an encouraging note of respect, offering the self-respect she had always hoped for.

Gina shared a house with a couple of people. Her room was rather plain, but she liked that; it allowed her to think clearly, an uncluttered space. The single bed emulated her life at that time. She contacted her family in Italy once a fortnight for about ten minutes: it was all she could afford. The coins would be gobbled up eagerly every couple of minutes. The telephone was on a small table in the hall and she would sit on the floor in an attempt to make herself comfortable while she chatted to her parents and sister and anyone who might be at the house, so far away. Its appetite for money reminded her of a creature she had once read about, a shrew in America that needs lots of food to keep its phenomenal metabolism going. Every day it would eat three times its own weight. Her eating habits were minimal in contrast, a crisp sandwich grabbed hastily on her way out, an apple or other piece of fruit, and then maybe a few biscuits with her coffee at work. In the evening, she would allow herself at least half an hour, to cook up some rice, with any leftover vegetables, usually carrots, which she would enjoy with a small glass of wine or water, depending on her finances that week.

She had had a few dates and her last boyfriend had moved in and stayed for almost a month, but struggling in a single bed and sharing a house was a problem for him. He wanted them to get their own place. By the time Gina had considered this as a possibility, he had left, bored with trying to fit into her zealous workload.

She was too busy for relationships, but police work was what she always wanted to do and she loved the exciting buzz of London. She often longed for home, for Italy, as anyone longs for the comforts of home and family when they are sitting quietly, alone and far away from family and friends. When it rained incessantly, she was usually busy in the office and hardly noticed, and whenever she had a week's holiday, her parents would help her with the flight back to Italy. Here she would relax and soak up the sun, but by the end of the week, she would be keen to get back to the job she loved.

The opportunity to go back to Italy and to work excited her and the inspector had promised to give her a day off to visit her home, just outside Florence.

The villa in Tuscany was struggling with the invasion of the police. Allen was in London again, sorting out their finances with the bank and raising a small loan to help them through the interim period. Rosemary had been busy making beds and helping Anna with the cleaning, when there was a forceful knock at the door. She turned impulsively to establish the source of this untimely intrusion, to see the police standing there. They had a few guests returning after the initial uproar; a small area was now cordoned off behind some temporary fencing and the gardens were showing some normality. The pool had been cleaned and they were feeling some sense of relief in the last couple of weeks. Her disappointment was evident in her brusque manner as she opened the door. The two men looked threatening in their appearance but the smaller man whom she recognised from previous visits had a softer edge, which settled her. Behind them a middle-aged man in a black raincoat and a younger woman were making their way up the jagged stone steps.

The Italian officers introduced the English inspector and his officer, Gina contributing to the conversation with a fluent flurry of Italian. Rosemary smiled nervously and replied in English to the relief of the inspector. She welcomed them in.

"We just need to ask you a few more questions, to clarify details gathered by the local police," Ian reassured her.

"I understand. I'm not sure I can help, but of course we'd like to get this resolved as soon as possible. It's really bad for business," she added, keeping the annoyance from showing in her rather clipped comment. Although Gina was left to sit quietly, observing the scene, she was attentive, considering the conversation carefully. She knew the inspector, 'Ian', as he insisted she call him, had been extremely grateful that she was able to study the case notes and translate for him when teasing information from the Italian Police. So far they had gathered the following facts: the owners Rosemary and Allen Richardson had moved to the villa a couple of years before the woman had been killed. They had established that the bush growing over the dead body had been planted about the same time the 'grave' had been dug. They had identified the body and they were now investigating possible suspects.

"Can I ask if you planted this shrub?" Gina leant over and showed them a picture of the camellia. Rosemary glanced at it, although she was well aware of the plant they were referring to.

"Yes, I did, when I landscaped the garden after the pool was built."

"Did anyone else help you with the garden?" More cautiously, she nodded. "A friend who was staying, Marjorie Birch."

"What about your husband?"

"No. He arrived back from London after their visit."

She was about to add more information about how her marriage worked, but decided it was none of their business. The death of their child had affected them both and they had dealt with it in their own way, even if to some their marriage seemed rather cold and unusual. She answered the questions honestly and succinctly but did not offer further details or elaborate, which she knew irritated the man in front of her. He continued to ascertain the information previously gathered by the local Italian Carabinieri. Rosemary was aware that she and her husband were suspects in this crime and she was careful not to incriminate herself or anyone else. It had been an idyllic holiday for her friends, and she treasured the memory. This had nothing to do with them and she hated the way the holiday was being tarnished by these intruders. When they finally left, Rosemary rubbed her hands nervously and picked up the telephone. She had not concerned anyone in England with the gruesome goings-on in Italy, but too many of the questions were leading towards that holiday. She realised her family and friends would soon be involved in the investigations.

"Penny, it's Rosemary, something terrible has happened." Penny's first thought was that something had happened to Geoff.

"A body has been found in our garden and the police are digging everything up. Everything is getting ruined and I don't know what we're going to do." Penny was never one for drama queens, but Rosemary had always been so together and unfazed. She went quiet and for once had no idea what to say.

"Bloody hell!" was the only response she could think of. Penny listened as Rosemary unravelled the facts, which sounded more like an Agatha Christie plot than a genuine narrative. "And I need to talk to Marjorie and Jim. It happened about the time they stayed." This last comment made Penny more uncomfortable. They had had enough problems to deal with. She wasn't sure how Marjorie would react.

"Let me talk to them. Is there anything in particular I need to tell them or ask them?"

"The police are asking about the camelia we planted. There was a piece of earth that had been newly dug over. I thought Marjorie had prepared the ground for planting, but it was where the body was buried. I haven't said anything to the police about why I chose that spot. Did they notice anything while they were staying? The police are going to turn up sooner or later and start asking questions."

"I'll have a chat with Marjorie and ring you back. Bloody hell."

Penny's first thought was to call Rosie. She was not sure how Marjorie would react, and she felt more comfortable addressing her niece over such a delicate matter. Penny felt her stomach twist, leaving a dull ache as she thought about the horror behind the brief telephone conversation. Over the past year, the three of them had built up a close bond and dealt with all sorts of problems, putting the world to rights. There was a solid friendship between Rosemary, Penny and Marjorie, and she somehow felt responsible for her sister-in-law and niece. She imagined the beautiful Tuscan property being ripped apart outside, an unpleasant panic creeping in. She couldn't think how any of this could involve the people she loved so dearly.

CHAPTER 16

Sam used to catch the bus to the station after school on the Friday and the train to London to visit his grandmother. His dad would drive up on Saturday morning and take him back with him. He was still quite young to be travelling alone, but he had completed the journey a couple of times before with his sister, and his parents encouraged his sense of adventure. He was often restless and out and about anyway. At least when he was with his grandmother or with his friend Paul, they knew where he was and what he was doing. Sam used to invite Paul round but now the house was sold. Now he went straight to Paul's, passing his grandparents' house that still held so many happy memories. It looked different. The new owners had changed the front door and repainted it. The lovely hydrangea had been dug up and concreted over, with simple pots and shrubs and room to park a car.

The last time he visited Paul, he was not his usual self and he did not want to go out. It was unlike his friend to be snappy. Paul told him that he had been skiving school lately, that he was feeling stressed about exams and did not see much of a future ahead of him. He was obviously a bit depressed and Sam worked hard to lighten his mood. Paul slung on a pair of jeans and a creased T-shirt, and they wandered off down to the park.

"It's alright for you. You'll be alright, you've got a family and a mum to look after you!" It was the first time Paul had ever shown such envy for his "neat life", as he called it and Sam was taken aback.

"Sometimes I wish I had a bit more time on my own and less fussing." His words held some truth. He knew he did have a nice house and loving family, unlike Paul, but his comment soothed the tension and Paul apologised for being such a 'moody git'!

"I've just been missing my mum lately. Sometimes wish I had a dad, even if he knocked me about a bit like Terry's dad. My aunt is brilliant, she is my mum really, but I get a bit lonely because she works most of the time. I'm glad you came round. You're an annoying prat sometimes, but a good mate." He kicked him playfully and then got out a packet of cigarettes for them to share while they walked back to the house.

Sam had enjoyed his brief time with his mate, despite Paul's outburst, and on Tuesday he had had a productive day at school. He had nearly finished his woodwork project and was feeling pleased with the clock he was making. He had decided to give it to his friend on his next visit. He was quiet and thoughtful in his room, when the telephone rang that evening. It was Paul, for Sam. Rosie knew she needed to confide in him now about the images that had bothered her since Sunday night. Rosie was sitting on the end of his bed, fanning through his comics, anticipating his return. Sam gave her a look of annoyance when he opened the door to his room, seeing her there, interrupting his privacy and looking at his things, but his thoughts were on the telephone conversation he had just had with Paul.

"It's Paul's mum. They have just found her body..." He trailed off, his eyes fixed on his sister. "What do you know, Rosie?"

"Not much...I haven't been able to 'see' much for a while. And I didn't know where you were or who you were with, when you went missing – even if you think I did," she added defiantly.

"Okay...okay but you must know something or you wouldn't be sitting on my bed! What the hell is going on?"

His mum had hovered in the hall when Sam was speaking to Paul and he'd told her to go away. It was private. That had not helped much. Most of the time his parents either ignored him, smothered him or just shouted at him anyway. The family seemed to be struggling its way through a heavy bag of washing that had an odious smell and no one wanted to deal with it. For the first time in a long time the two siblings sat close, holding each other's hands, grief and worry wrapping them in a transparent shawl.

Despite the rift that had grown between them over the last couple of years, Rosie was at ease at that moment with her young brother as she focused on the images and ideas that had brought her to him with such an alarming force. The body she described to Sam could quite easily be that of Paul's mother, which would explain her belief that Paul was involved. But her fears for her father did not make sense. There was no connection between Paul's family and hers, except that Paul and Sam were friends. Paul's mother had disappeared years ago with her boyfriend. Both Paul and his aunt had lost contact with her. Sam knew this of course and, although his friend was nonchalant about it, he suspected Paul was suffering, feeling abandoned and angry, suppressing the hate he felt for the man she went off with and upset that his mother never felt the need to keep in touch. His outburst during his 'visit', had confirmed his suspicions that Paul was quite troubled by this desertion. His aunt had said she'd been brainwashed by this Gavin, and the two sisters had fallen out in an explosion of hateful, stinging words, so when they left the country – America, Sam had been told, he accepted the situation with an abruptness that surprised everyone and moved on. His aunt was a great mum and he was popular at school, with friends to distract him and make him feel like he belonged. The shock he now felt was partly disbelief and partly guilt that he had no idea she'd been dead for such a long time – about ten years in fact, about the time contact ceased. His aunt was too distraught to talk to him and Paul turned to Sam for some sort of support and reconciliation.

"He wants me to go and stay for a few days."

"But you can't, you'll be needed here."

"I know that!" He spat the words out in annoyance. Rosie realised then that she needed to take some control. She left her brother slumped on the bed and went to talk to her mother. Perhaps her visions were trying to encourage her family to help in some way. She was finding it very difficult to read her thoughts. Perhaps she was trying too hard.

Marjorie was just putting the butter in the pan of boiled potatoes, ready to mash; sausages and mash were her dad's favourite.

"Mum?" she spoke with some caution before suggesting that Sam invite his friend Paul down from London. He'd just found out his mum had died abroad and that perhaps they, particularly Sam, could offer him some support for a few days.

"Hasn't he got any other friends? What about his aunt?"

"I just think it's a good idea." Rosie spoke with a firmness that her mother hadn't recognised for a while.

"Well, okay, if you think it's best…" She would never argue with her daughter's intuition, but this strange and unexpected request made her feel very awkward and a little concerned; she had no idea why. Jim would be home soon, and he could make the final decision. "But we will have to check with your father."

Just as Rosie was about to make her way upstairs to seek out her brother, the telephone rang again: it was her Auntie Penny.

Events had been tumbling towards her at such a speed in the last few hours, she hardly had time to consider the thoughts and images that kept fighting her for attention, and when she did, she was confused and disorientated. She picked up the telephone, half-expecting to hand it over to her mother, when she realised who was calling.

"No, Rosie, I want to talk to you, if that's okay."

"Of course, but can we talk another time, it's a bit awkward at the moment?"

"It's important, Rosie. I need to talk to you about your parents."

"Hold on, Auntie, there's someone at the door." She put the receiver down on the telephone table and went to answer it, while her mother was dishing up dinner. It was probably her dad, due home any minute. She wasn't sure why he'd knocked. He always had his key. She could detect two people. He must have brought someone back with him. But when she opened the door, a woman police officer and someone who looked a bit like a detective stood firmly on the doorstep.

"Just dishing up, darling," her mother called from the kitchen.

"It's not Dad. It's the police," Rosie called back.

"We have a few questions to ask your father, Mr James Birch," the man informed her.

"I know." She spoke these words confidently without realising their significance. "He's not home yet. He should be home in a minute," Rosie addressed the visitors and let them in. She put the telephone receiver back down without speaking, leaving Penny hanging on the other end, wondering if they'd been cut off, but fearing the worst, sure that she heard the words "the police" in the background.

James Birch was cautioned and arrested that evening for the murder of Lucy Jameson. They hadn't even sat down for tea. Marjorie was asked to go to the station in the morning, for now she sat frightened and shocked, comforted by her daughter and son, her children sitting like stuffed dolls beside her. Their mother suddenly turned to Rosie.

"Rosie, you need to use your gift if you still have it. You need to find out what happened."

Of course, she and Sam had already come to this conclusion. Paul staying seemed to be out of the question now, but they needed to talk to him.

News of Jim's arrest shocked everyone, but instead of being ostracised, help and sympathy flooded in from neighbours and friends. No one believed he had been involved and even Inspector Graham was not convinced they had the right man, but the facts were there in black and white. Marjorie's statement only reinforced what they already knew. The Birches were staying at the Tuscan villa at the time of the murder. Everyone had gone out the day the earth had been dug over, instigating the planting of the shrub in that exact spot – everyone, that is, except for James Birch, who had been left alone nearly all day, by the pool, just a few yards from where the body was buried. He had known the victim well – very well – although it had been years ago. She must have met up with him, they fought, and he killed her. Part of one of the fingerprints they were able to rescue was a similar match to his. There seemed to be little doubt. Who else could it have been? There was no one else there in this remote part of Tuscany.

PART TWO

CHAPTER 1

As soon as she walked into the office, Lucy liked the look of the man at the desk. His dark brown eyes looked up at her and he smiled warmly, showing his obvious approval.

"You must be Lucy, the new secretary." He stood up to welcome her, offering a firm handshake and smiling again. She was startled by her impulsive attraction towards him, wanting to kiss that mouth.

"Yes. You must be Mr Birch." She steadied her voice, but spoke with softness, to tempt his interest. She tried her rather sexy, winning smile. She was glad she'd worn the silkier, cream blouse that neatly showed off her breasts.

"Call me Jim. That will be your desk and I have already drafted some letters for typing."

Sitting back down at his own desk, he didn't seem to notice her attempts at engaging him. She would try harder later: now wasn't the time. She would work on impressing him with her typing skills. She knew she was an excellent secretary. She'd passed all her tests at the Pitman's College with distinctions. This was her first job, but she intended to climb the ladder quickly. She was ambitious and clever.

The time went by quickly; there was plenty to do and

when she had completed all the typing, Jim Birch had asked if she could organise the filing cabinet. "Bring some order to the chaos," he had said. Inside, that was exactly what she was trying to do with her feelings, bring some order and control to her chaotic heartbeat. He hadn't spoken much, except to give some advice and explain what was expected. His instructions were clear and formal, but she was sure he liked her. He smiled a lot. Perhaps he was a bit shy. She could be quite overpowering with men and she knew most men found her confidence and sexiness rather overwhelming. She decided his lack of interest was not because he didn't fancy her, but rather that he must be married.

Over the first couple of weeks, Lucy worked on building up their friendship and finding out more about her delicious boss. She was so efficient he seemed more relaxed in his work and found more time to chat. Jim found himself whistling on his way to work and staying a bit later, enjoying the company of his new secretary. His wife was often too tired or irritable lately to enjoy the easy banter he and Lucy enjoyed in the office. He was definitely attracted to this sexy young woman. It wasn't long before he found himself asking her out for drink and something to eat, in the pub nearby, at lunchtime. He convinced himself it was a reward for all her hard work. It was one harmless drink.

Lucy knew he was hooked as soon as they left the office to enjoy a drink and a pub lunch. They walked side by side, aware of the purposeful gap between them. As they reached the heavy wooden door, he moved forward swiftly to hold it open, laying his hand gently in the small of her back as she went in. They sat in a booth in the corner and as he leant over to pass her the menu, she looked up and moved in to brush a confident kiss on his mouth, just missing his lips. It was a small, calculated action that had the desired effect. He looked at her now with lustful eyes, concern and guilt nagging him, as he thought briefly about his wife and children at home.

Although he desired Lucy, he was reluctant to get involved, but she was so persuasive, and he felt so vulnerable. He allowed their relationship to develop steadily. He was very careful in his deceit, but he knew Marjorie had become suspicious, and when she turned on him one evening and asked, "Are you having an affair?" he was unable to deny it. He realised then he was about to lose the only woman he would ever really love and, even worse, lose his children.

"I'm sorry. I love you, Marjorie. It was a mistake. Please forgive me." Jim seemed to crumble into the settee, suddenly aware of the relief his admission had brought. What was he thinking? How could he have been so stupid? There was an awkward, unpleasant growth lingering between them now. He felt its destructive influence and it was all his fault. He broke down and wept. Marjorie's silent grief broke into a quiet whimpering and she sat beside him, holding onto her husband now, allowing the panic and anger to subside.

She loved this man. He was her world and she forgave him.
His promise to end the affair was determined, although he
knew he would be less confident in his determination when
confronted by Lucy. He would look for a new position,
enquire about a move to one of the other offices, or work on
some other resolution. The following week he was tidying
his desk. He had been offered a sideways move to an office
a further twelve miles away and in less than a month he
had almost forgotten all about Lucy.

CHAPTER 2

When Lucy arrived at work, she could feel the tension in the small office as soon as she opened the door.

"Marjorie knows. I need to end it." The words were obviously rehearsed and there was a hardness in his voice. Lucy stood glaring at him in disbelief. She loved him. What did he think he was saying? He couldn't possibly mean it. She felt her knees weaken and sat down, staring at him in shock. She had no words, no reply and then the tears exploded, uncontrolled and exhausting. She tried to cling to him then and pleaded like a child. He was embarrassed now.

"You should go home. Take the day off. I'm sorry, Lucy." He really was sorry, but she must have known it was just a fling. Lucy left, grabbing her bag in a trance-like state, and walked out of the office.

She was devastated and now she was angry. After taking a few days off, to lie in bed, sleeping and crying, until she felt able to wander around her flat and avoid the alcohol for a little food, she made her way to the place that held so much hope, to hand her notice in. She felt nauseous and didn't think she would ever get over him. Her sister had been brilliant, supporting her as well as giving her enough space to mend. She even took a few days off work to be with her. She'd get another job, start again, but the tight knot in her stomach refused to disperse and the sickness she was feeling nagged at her constantly. When a few weeks later she realised she was pregnant, she became totally dependent on her sister and moved to be with her in London.

Julie's flat was only one bedroom and the thought of a baby inhabiting the small space was worrying. She was completing her last year as a trainee nurse and would soon be able to consider buying a small place of her own. Lucy's dramatic arrival was totally unexpected. When Julie's doorbell rumbled pathetically, it took a few moments for her to recognise this unfamiliar sound. She worked hard, lived alone and was not accustomed to visitors.

"Lucy!" the surprise was noted.

"Oh Julie!"

She fell into her sister's arms, like a small, bereft child, clinging nervously and weeping tears as part of her dramatic entry. Julie was annoyed by her sister's unnecessary behaviour but let her play her part for effect. She knew her games and, although they irritated her, she was aware that she had encouraged such behaviour by spoiling her and allowing her to command every situation, from a very young age. She settled to the practicalities of dealing with Lucy's situation in the efficient and adult way she tackled all of life's difficulties. And this was what Lucy had hoped for. She needed Julie.

"If you are going to stay and bring up your baby on your own, perhaps we should consider buying a bigger place together," she had suggested. Julie had tried to convince Lucy to tell the father and get some financial support. He needed to face his responsibilities, but Lucy was effusive. She wanted nothing to do with him. She wouldn't even mention his name.

The protective, motherly instincts Julie felt for her younger sister were obviously a result of her upbringing. Her mother was very young when she had Julie, only sixteen in fact. Her mother enjoyed partying, and from the one photograph they had of her when she was young, she had clearly been a beauty. Julie was in foster care for at least four years before her mother was ready to have her back, and any bond that might have been established between mother and daughter had been lost along the way. When her sister Lucy was born a year later, much of her childhood was spent looking after the baby, while her mother was out working or enjoying herself. She didn't really feel anything for this woman who had given birth to her, but she loved Lucy. There was never a father figure in her life; a few men arrived, became 'uncle' and then left again. And of course, her mother's friends were transient because of her rather promiscuous lifestyle. Now looking at her sister, sitting in a dreamlike state, defenceless again, she felt the urge to support and love her with a determination and duty, whatever the circumstances. Lucy, being Lucy, showed very little thanks; she expected it and she had mastered the art of manipulation with great success. She lacked any interest in the baby she was carrying; in fact it caused her more pain to know it belonged to the man she loved and could not have. Her jealousy against his wife and other children was simmering like a time bomb.

It was a beautiful spring morning when Paul was born. She had awoken at about four o'clock, groaning and complaining of an incessant pain in her back. Julie had only been home a couple of hours from a long shift and rolled over, letting out her own annoyed groan, partly from her tired state, partly from Lucy's demanding neediness.

"Go and have a hot bath or make a cup of tea," Julie suggested; one of many statements of advice given to her by Shirley, a trainee midwife, who seemed as excited about Julie becoming an auntie as Julie had been.

Regaining her senses from the sleepy stupor she was fighting, she climbed out of bed to aid her sister, who was now pacing up and down and grumbling.

"Are you excited?"

"No!" She spoke sharply. "I don't want this stupid baby!" and she began to cry; those familiar tears of disappointment, so childlike and forced. Men loved this weak and frail dependence. Her sister shrugged it off easily. With her usual accommodating manner, she gathered up her sister and the small case she'd packed and her sister.

"Come on, we're going to the hospital," secretly loving every minute and aroused by the prospect of becoming an auntie. After all, caring for others was her profession; it had been her life; it was all she knew.

Although Lucy loved the tiny boy snuggled in her arms, she tired easily and she was keen to ween him off breast milk and give him a bottle. This, Lucy had calculated, would allow her to have more freedom. Her elder sister could babysit more and she could get back to work. Women these days were becoming much more independent. There were numerous possibilities for secretaries. You could work and be a mother, too, and that is what she wanted. She didn't want to stay too long cooped up in her sister's claustrophobic flat!

Julie loved the little bundle. She'd looked after her mother and her young sister and caring for others was her career choice; caring for little Paul came naturally. Her sister preferred to go out and socialise and now she was looking to have a career. Lucy wanted to move out of the tiny flat and she hated spending so much of her hard-earned money on bills. Julie was constantly juggling her life between nursing shifts and looking after her nephew. It was tiresome but she was determined to make things work for her family. There were intimate evenings between the two sisters when Paul was tucked up safely in his small bed, fitted snuggly beside the single bed her sister occupied. They had bought a sofa bed for Julie to sleep on; it was comfy enough and after a while the compact space no longer seemed to bother her. Even when Paul was clambering around as a healthy two-year-old, they managed.

The park opposite became his playground most days until he was placed safely in the compounds of Mrs Smith, the childminder across the road. Lucy loved him, but usually only enjoyed the joys of motherhood when it suited her. Julie and Lucy had several arguments over Paul and the atmosphere would become quite strained as he approached his third birthday.

"I thought we could book the local community hall, for his birthday."

"Won't that cost a lot?"

"Not much and we could decorate it with balloons and bunting and invite his friends."

"He hasn't got many." Lucy's negativity was deflating Julie's enthusiasm.

"It will be fun." She continued to work on her sister, until Lucy turned on her vehemently.

"No! He's not your son. It's too much money and I want to take him out for the day, to the zoo maybe."

She spoke with a childish jealousy. "Because it was easier," Julie thought. Lucy reminded her sister often that he was her son, something she tended to forget when she relied on her sister to pick him up or look after him, when she had a busy schedule. Despite their genuinely friendly, sisterly moments, arguments had flared up regularly lately. They were close to falling out entirely, when she brought Gavin back to the flat one evening.

CHAPTER 3

Lucy had met Gavin in a department store: he was buying some aftershave, and she had been smelling the perfumes. She knew he had been watching her, but she was used to men admiring her. He had very sexy, penetrating, dark brown eyes and for a moment he reminded her of Jim, except he was much taller and his hair was sleeker, almost shiny. He came up behind her as she stood at the till and placed his arm around her lightly.

"You know, you are very beautiful," he murmured confidently. He was dressed in a smart, quality suit: the crisp, white shirt and navy, striped tie were tickled by his dark, slightly curling hair. She found herself admiring his rather controlling confidence.

"Thank you," she said, acknowledging his remark. He carried her bag to the car and without hesitation asked her out. The date was a complete success. They talked with ease and he threw money about with a reassuring arrogance that made him even more attractive. He was in business and he had his own expensive, four-bedroomed property in Chelsea. His car was a sporty Ferrari. Wow, Lucy couldn't believe her luck. She kept him secret from

171

her sister because she didn't expect the relationship to last. She knew he could have anyone he wanted. For some reason he seemed besotted with her.

Lucy sat on her small bed, painting her nails with the new, bright polish she had treated herself to, in the same department store which had introduced her to her wealthy boyfriend. She glanced over at Paul, playing quietly with some bricks beside her. She really did love the little boy, but she was not a confident mother. Despite her independence, she was aware of how much she relied on her sister and how fond of her nephew Julie was. Lucy was aware that, despite her confident persona, she was bored with the selfish independence she had built her life on, and what she really wanted was a home for her, her son and a husband. If she couldn't have Jim, there was Gavin. He could certainly provide for them and he was desperately in love with her. That seemed to be the plan evolving in her mind, even though she recognised that Julie loved being a family of three and would miss them terribly. But as yet Gavin didn't know of Paul's existence. She hadn't wanted to spoil the fun she was having and ruin everything, not until she knew whether this wonderful man might be understanding of her situation. After a few weeks, fairly confident their relationship might survive her guilty confession, she braved the conversation that she had been working on in her mind over dessert at Gavin's favourite restaurant.

"I have something I must tell you." She paused

awkwardly. He leant across and took her hand gently, caressing her fingers.

"I have a son," she blurted out. Her eyes were alert, looking for some sign of what his response might be. She suddenly felt uncomfortable and unsure of his reaction, trying not to spoil what had been a wonderful evening.

"It's okay…I love you."

Lucy was aware of some reservation in his words, but she was focused on the words, "I love you," and that sent her into a whirlwind of ecstasy. How could she possibly be so lucky? This rich, handsome man loved her. That evening, she took him back to meet her sister, her expectations high.

Julie's first impressions of her sister's boyfriend were mixed. He was handsome, slightly older than she would have hoped for Lucy, but obviously rich. He held Lucy's hand with real tenderness and constantly watched her sister with his adoring eyes. He seemed totally absorbed. But there was something about him that unnerved her. He was perhaps too attentive, too adoring. She thought maybe she might be jealous and dismissed these doubts as they settled like a warning. Ignoring her troubled feelings, she welcomed him into their lives with an animated generosity: after all, she didn't have to worry about her future anymore. He would look after Lucy and Paul; she could buy that little place of her own that she had set her heart on and she anticipated the regular babysitting duties her sister would demand of her. She would still be an important part of their lives. It seemed perfect.

Although Julie began to spend more of her time off, looking after Paul, she told herself that Lucy had a chance of love and a successful career, which would provide a stable home for her son. Her sacrifices now would help her secure a future in which they would all benefit. Paul was easy, too. In fact, he seemed more at ease in her company than he did with his own mother sometimes. When her sister suddenly announced she wanted to go on holiday with Gavin and could she look after Paul for a few days, Julie agreed reluctantly and booked some more time off work.

"I don't know what I'd do without you. Thank you. I'm lucky to have you as my sister."

Lucy grinned. It was a generous and heartfelt sentiment, slightly unusual for her sister and it caught Julie off guard.

Lucy seemed to be on a roller coaster, enjoying parties, dressing up in beautiful furs and gowns, spoilt and treated like a child at Christmas, and now she was off to a Spanish island for a short break with her handsome boyfriend. Her career ambitions were on hold because he had given her so much. He made her wonder why she needed to work. She followed him around from one exciting event to another and then busied herself in his home with meals and sexual temptations whenever he returned from a business venture. She spent a few days enjoying her son, taking him out and about in the car Gavin had bought her; his car was understandably for his use only. It wasn't until she kissed her little son and hugged him 'goodbye', to climb into the taxi for her trip abroad, that she suddenly felt a sense of trepidation. Gavin had almost taken over her life, her being, and she suddenly felt an uncomfortable pull towards this little boy; a fleeting sense that she was losing her son.

Gavin was not very interested in Paul and almost humoured her own part as a mother. She looked over at her sister, standing holding her son comfortably, and felt a loss, a longing for a simpler life, a life which she controlled, where she was a major player. Her doubts were disturbed as the taxi driver called to her with a sense of urgency and she picked up her case, avoiding the questions forming in her mind. When she returned home with a wedding ring on her finger, she had no idea why she'd agreed to marry him. It was as if her life was being mapped out and she was a princess, following the rules to enjoy the pleasures. He'd organised the whole thing: the romantic meal, her wedding dress, the flowers and the quiet venue, with a few friends in a luxurious hotel. She hadn't really noticed Gavin's jealous tendencies until their wedding night.

She came out of the bathroom in the delicate negligée that he'd chosen for her, wafting sensually towards the bed.

"You look beautiful," he simmered. He was a good lover but tonight he seemed less concerned with pleasuring her.

His gentle, warm lips that often caressed her nipples and thighs were harder and more demanding. He seemed hungry almost for her body and then afterwards turned over to sleep with an unsettling abandonment. It was probably the strain of the day, and of course now that they were married they could be together whenever they wished. She suddenly realised at that moment that she did not wish to be with him and a longing for Jim returned, unsettling her further. "Damn it!" she thought. "Why did he still continually invade her thoughts?" She knew why. She still loved him.

CHAPTER 4

Paul had two particular memories of his mother; he remembered her climbing into a shiny, black sports car. Her hair had been cut into a harsh bob and he didn't like it. She had been away a lot over the last couple of years. Today it felt different. She had a much larger case and she had given him a much longer hug. His mum and auntie had had a huge row last night and he'd listened to the tears. Angry words had resonated through the small house they had moved into a few months ago, "to have more space" so that "they could be secure as a family", his aunt's words kicking at his senses, the irony evident as his small family fell apart. "It was all Gavin's fault!" The words thundering in his head and not quite making it out of his mouth.

Julie was used to her sister's whimsical visits now, depositing her son like a heavy package. Gavin had no time for Paul and she was aware of the conflict this was causing between them. Lucy was aware that Paul was happier with her sister, but she was his mother. But Paul recognised her now, as someone who just dropped in occasionally to shower him with loving words and wistful longing, before rushing off on some jaunt across the world with her husband. His last memory of his mother was a few months later. She had been talking to him about his new friend, Sam. He remembered babbling on in an excited, tumultuous flow of words. He remembered this moment particularly, because she was listening, really listening, not like any other time he could remember.

When the letters and phone calls stopped, Paul was only seven years old. At first Julie was not overly concerned. But after several weeks, she decided to try to make contact. The phone number Lucy had given her was a dead end. The woman's recorded voice at the other end repeatedly informed her that the number "has not been recognised". She wrote to both of the addresses, the one in London and the other in Paris, addresses that she had found under several notes in a desk drawer. Then she waited for a reply. She tried to ignore her nagging concerns and focused on Paul. He was her priority now, but her motherly instincts towards her sister created a sickness she could not shift. It wasn't until now that she realised she knew very little about her sister's husband. His name was Gavin – Gavin Jameson, her sister's new surname. She didn't know who he worked for or why they travelled so much, and, although she had these contact addresses, she had never visited them. She had only been out with them once, on her sister's birthday – she had insisted. She knew he was controlling and quite jealous of her son. They had had many rows over the fact. She realised now she had never liked the man, but he was her sister's husband. After nearly two months, with no reply from her letters, she decided to visit the London address. Paris was out of the question!

She studied the map, tracing her finger along the roads to find Chelsea. It was across the other side of London, an area she was unfamiliar with. She'd find a newsagent's or maybe a police station, and ask for instructions, once she got there. It was a Thursday. Paul was at school and it was her day off.

The roads were reasonably quiet. Except for a milk van cutting her up and causing her to just miss a lamp-post, it was an uneventful journey. Her mind continued to wander: what would she say? What would she do once she got there? What would her sister say? Pulling her attention back to the traffic and the roads, she finally arrived. She was considering where to stop, who to ask for directions, when she noticed the sign: 'Police Station'. It was as if fate had placed it there for her convenience. Following the sign's direction down two busy roads, she pulled up outside, in a small car park.

The policeman at the desk seemed amused by her story and a little flippant. He saw her as a fussy housewife with nothing better to do than chase round the country, making a nuisance of herself. He asked her a few questions and wrote down some vague notes. He flicked through some pages of a directory and went to a filing cabinet and then another. He looked quizzically at his notes and asked her the same questions again, to check the details.

"Well, there is an Abingdon Road in Chelsea, but no four-bedroomed houses and no number 203. And there are a few G. Jamesons, but none living in that area. I'm afraid you are mistaken."

"My sister has been gone nearly two months. This is the address I have for her." She was about to mention Paul, but thought better of it. She wasn't his mother. It might complicate things – cause trouble.

"Do you want me to register her as a missing person, madam?"

"No, it's okay. I'm sure she'll contact me soon."

"That's the trouble with families; always rowing, always taking off!"

Julie did not respond. The anxiety she felt, mixed with the need to avoid trouble for her sister and her nephew, prevented her from saying any more. She didn't like him or his attitude anyway.

She didn't remember much about the journey back, her tears and emotions covering her in a cloak of invisibility as she drove, almost in a trance. By the time she opened her front door, she had resigned herself to carry on as normal and wait. There was very little else she could do. As the months rolled by and the years followed, she let go. Her sister was obviously living her life somewhere with Gavin and had abandoned her son for her husband. Bitter and hurt, she hid her feelings deep in the recesses of her heart, only opening doors to offer love and protection for her nephew – her son, as far as everyone around her was concerned.

Paul stopped longing for his mother years ago. He knew he loved her because she was his mum, but it was obvious she loved Gavin more and had never really wanted him. He and his auntie were a team. They loved each other, and he told himself that was good enough. His friendship with Sam had come along just at the right time. She didn't come back, but Sam had arrived like an unexpected younger brother – and he was having fun.

When the police knocked on their door, Paul climbed out of bed reluctantly. He had just turned eighteen and was working shifts at the local factory. He was supposed to be having a well-earned lie-in and was not impressed at being disturbed. They could be calling for a number of reasons: the weed he had been smoking, the car he nicked to drive home the other week, or the fight he had in town a couple of months ago, but these were just small incidents. Perhaps it had something to do with one of the girls he had dated. There were two of them and he suddenly felt uneasy.

"Is your aunt here?" the woman asked congenially. Paul was confused. What would the police want with his hard-working, law-abiding aunt?

"Er…no. She's at work."

"Are you Paul Jameson?" It had been a very long time since he had heard that name and the shocked look was picked up immediately by the two officers regarding him carefully.

"No. My name is Paul Thomas. Jameson is my mother's married name." The woman officer made a few scribbled notes in her book. The man, obviously in charge because she kept glancing over to him for some sort of approval, stood firmly beside her, allowing her to ask the questions. Moving forward now he spoke clearly and with a firmness that unnerved him. Paul was quite big for his age, good-looking, confident and not to be intimidated, but the name 'Jameson' had knocked him like a fist to the jaw. He seemed to shrink in front of them and was finding it hard to speak at all.

"Can we come in?"

"Why?" It was a natural remark, reflecting his confusion. He was feeling defensive.

"We have found a body and we think it is your mother."

The words did not register fully at first. He was stunned into a dramatic and uncomfortable silence. He didn't remember the phone call to his aunt; he didn't remember much about the moments that followed; he did remember sitting blankly, staring at the television silently reflecting his shadowed image on the blank, grey screen, while his aunt and the police gathered facts, working through questions and answers like a quiz show.

CHAPTER 5

Lucy was transfixed by the words she was hearing, as she listened to her son talking about his new friend, Sam. "His parents, Jim and Marjorie, are on holiday in Tuscany and he is staying with his grandparents a few doors up." She knew it was her Jim, the Jim she still loved: Paul's father. The longing she had kept hidden surfaced like a tidal wave, drowning her. She wanted him suddenly with a lustful energy that she was not prepared to control. He showed her the picture Sam had brought round of the Tuscan home, the address printed clearly on the back, as if for her. Paul knew Sam was rather envious of his parents' holiday and had shown him this, as evidence, when Paul had suggested his parents were unlikely to be going somewhere quite as exotic.

"My mother travels all the time and she has a place in Paris," he replied with a similar boast. Sam knew not to delve further. Paul was sensitive about his mother's life which did not seem to include him. When his mother gathered up her bag and a few things and left hurriedly, Paul watched her go, with the usual sense of loss and abandonment. He picked up the picture, screwed it up and threw it across the room.

That afternoon, Sam came around and they went off to the park and Paul thought nothing more of the incident.

The police asked a few more questions, but his aunt's obvious distress and Paul's own disbelief and shock were preventing them from making much progress.

"When you are feeling a bit better, perhaps you and your nephew can pop into the station to answer a few more questions," the woman officer suggested. She hesitated and looked across at the inspector, leaving him to state the more pressing matter.

"We will also need one of you to come in and identify the body…"

"We'll both come in," Paul offered, not quite sure if this was actually what he wanted, but his aunt's grief was obvious. She couldn't do this on her own. A noticeable relief was evident as they walked out of the front door, but his aunt erupted into a fit of tears. Paul suddenly felt awkward and in need of his friend. He picked up the telephone and rang Sam.

Julie had been too distraught to work and hardly left her bedroom for three days; however, by the fourth day she was up, had returned to work and was acting as if nothing had happened. Paul knew this was her way of coping, but a strange rift had developed between them. He was like his mother to look at, he knew; it had been commented on several times by different people. To his aunt he was a constant reminder of Lucy's death. When Sam's parents said he could stay with them, Paul knew it would be good for both of them. Julie had identified the body without him, suddenly one afternoon after work, and she had arranged for a second visit from the police, to answer further questions, the evening before Paul was to leave. They needed to know when and where he was going and the information she gave seemed to be of particular interest. The wall she was building between her and Paul was obviously a reaction to the loss of her sister, but Paul was now having to deal with the loss of his aunt's love, too. The distance between them was like a death itself, and Paul was hurting much more than he realised. He could not bring himself to speak of his feelings and suffered silently while he watched his aunt harden and busy herself into a life of denial.

The same police officers that had visited before entered with a friendly, warm and sympathetic manner and made themselves comfortable, like old friends. Then the questions started. They were focusing on her movements, the weeks leading up to the last time they had seen her. Her body had been found in Italy, Tuscany in fact, information that until now was unknown to either of them.

"How did she know about the Tuscan villa?" the woman officer interjected.

"I told her," Paul suddenly chipped in. The memory

escaping like a wild bird taking flight. The officers turned their attention towards him; his aunt turned to look quizzically at her nephew.

"You never mentioned anything." Annoyance was creeping into her voice.

"You knew I was worried about her. You never mentioned this all those years ago." Paul shrugged.

"You never asked. And I had forgotten." With the attention now firmly fixed on him, Paul deciphered the scattered memories and offered details once buried, now coming to the surface with unprecedented force. The woman continued to scribble notes, nodding at intervals as she proceeded to make some sense of his ramblings.

Julie was looking hard at Paul now. She was scratching around her own memories and finding no answers. The two of them had lived their own lives, letting Lucy live hers. The gap which had been growing between them lifted, creating a pathway back. She loved Paul: he had always been more of a son to her than his mother. They needed each other now. When they had gone, Paul and Julie moved close and hugged. The realisation that Lucy was dead sank in fully and, as it did, the tears faltered. Both felt sad. Both felt an incredible guilty loss, but both realised then that they had moved on and left her behind. They needed each other now.

"I'd rather you stayed here, with me." Julie's pleading tones resonating in the hallway.

"I know, but I really need to talk to Sam. His dad's

involved somehow. The police aren't telling us much. I'd like to know what's been going on. I'll just stay a few days. You've got work and I'm just sitting around doing nothing now that the manager at the factory has laid me off." His boss was not interested in Paul's business. He'd had too many days off and he'd been replaced. Now all he did was mope around, spending too much time thinking and not getting anywhere. He couldn't get on with his life. He was in limbo. He might not have missed his mother for several years, but now he knew it wasn't her choice; she must have loved him after all, and he wanted to know what had happened to her.

Lucy hesitated at the airport. She hadn't phoned Gavin. He would be wondering where she was. But she had to see Jim again. She wanted to tell him about Paul. She wanted him.

Gavin was watching. He was always watching. He followed her, bought a ticket on the same flight and watched her climb aboard and settle into her seat. He had no idea what she was doing but she wasn't going to do it, whatever it was, without him. It had been easy to follow her. "She used my damn credit card," he thought. "Stupid bitch!" The muttered words were spoken with vengeance.

The long walk up the hill was tiring. The dust and heat made her dry and uncomfortable. She pulled out the warm bottle of water from her bag and savoured the last few drops. The madness of the situation was questioning every step she took, but her determination propelled her forward.

And Gavin was not far behind.

An overgrown lane was hidden from view, until she was just yards from its opening, where it was cloaked in the branches of boxwood shrubs and surrounded by drying grasses, with a backdrop of more dark green cypresses. She had not intended to converse with the locals; her secrecy seemed paramount, but she was disorientated and dehydrated. She had no idea what she was doing here all alone: the only surety was her urge to see Jim. This urge overpowered logic, although at that moment it all seemed rather senseless. She had come this far, though, and there was no going back.

The lane would likely take her to a house or houses where she hoped she would find a friendly native, who would offer her water and a friendly welcome. She was in need of some local knowledge of the area and some support as the feeling of solitary abandonment increased her doubt and anxiety. At the end of the narrowing drive was a path, leading to the front door of a small, cottage-like home. Its walls were crumbling in parts and the shutters hung awkwardly on the rusted hinges. However, throbbing blue sky and the blossoming flowers splattered amongst the green, surrounding the rather dilapidated dwelling projected a homely invitation.

She stood nervously on the threshold and tapped on the door. Lucy waited for a moment, considering her options if there was no answer, when eventually the rattle of a gate, to her left, disturbed the silence. A woman in muddy boots and trousers, with dark, untamed hair, held back with a scarf, looked at the stranger with curiosity. The foreign words cascaded fluently, in a friendly tone, towards her, as she stepped forward.

"I'm English," she volunteered politely, waving her empty bottle hopefully. Immediately she regretted her words. She did not want anyone to know she was there. She had not intended to offer such information so openly. But what harm would it do? The woman was unlikely to speak to or see anyone. She lived alone, it seemed, away from the rest of the community, abandoned like her dishevelled home, at the bottom of a sparsely used lane. The woman waved her hands enthusiastically, beckoning her forwards through the gate and into a small room with a sink. Filling the bottle with water, she continued to speak, more slowly this time, in a beautiful, lilting, rhythmic sound which pleasantly captivated Lucy, though the meaning was lost in communication. Lucy nodded with a "Thank you" as the woman handed her back the bottle, showing her the picture of the villa and pointing to the address scrawled on the back. The woman waved her hands again, enthusiastically pointing to the left, then up and up and finally to the right.

With some confidence that this made sense and would help her reach her goal, Lucy nodded again with another "Thank you" and left, back down the lane and onto the path from which she had arrived. She turned left and made her way slowly up the incline of a rather steep hill. She could see nothing beyond, as it stretched up towards the expanse of blue sky, as if stretching up to the heavens. She paused at the top, arriving at a junction with two dirt tracks, surrounded by olive groves, one to the left and one to the right. She thought of the woman waving her hands to the right helpfully and drank generously from the bottle before taking that route.

Whether it was the refreshing water or a sudden driving compulsion to see Jim, she moved with renewed energy and determination. The path meandered like a snake, and she followed it, like a castaway on an uninhabited island. Finally, she turned a corner and spotted a villa in the distance; the villa in the picture.

It was quite large and had obviously been added onto, though tastefully, in a similar local brick. The front garden was welcoming, surrounded by a sturdy rock fortress, scattered with small evergreens and some well-positioned colourful flowering plants, similar to those she had encountered at the lonely dwelling where she had stopped. This pathway led up to large, wooden doors, which were painted affectionately in a complementary dark red. The path was marked with smooth, white stones, sympathetically chosen to entice guests up to the front door.

A truck was parked randomly outside, suggesting human activity somewhere inside or in the grounds, but the silence suggested otherwise. Lucy stood still, taking in her surroundings and noting any movement and activity, before venturing forwards to investigate. She watched two women appear at the doorway and watched them as they climbed into the truck and leave. She heard an old man call out from upstairs and then pull the shutters closed, retiring in his room for a siesta, and from her vantage point she could just see the edge of the pool and the feet of someone on a sunbed; that she thought must be Jim and her heart quickened. She waited for several minutes before moving from her hiding place.

CHAPTER 6

Paul caught the 9.30 train after rush hour. The damp air and cold mist were lifting, and a splash of blue was peeping through the dulled clouds. He had two stops before his own and time to reflect. Time which would alleviate the troubled and confused thoughts he was battling with. The carriage he picked was reasonably empty; the blue and green checked seats looked worn. But Paul was mesmerised by his own silence and planted himself by a window, opposite a nondescript woman reading a book. His gaze, disturbed by the mottled black, grubby marks on the window, barely registered the green fields rushing by. The smudges and, in particular, a small, black mark which stretched out from the corner helped him focus on nothing as he followed the stream of trees and shrubs speeding past, blurred green-grey and brown, washed-out lines of colour. He allowed his memories to bother him, slowly and distinctively, watching the action like a play rehearsal. Details altered but certain images repeated over and over. His emotions simmered.

The main question in his mind forced itself open constantly: "Why did his mother rush off to Tuscany and to her death?" Paul had been convinced that Gavin was involved in her murder, but his own animosity towards him may have clouded his judgement. If that was the case, why hadn't he come looking for her, or was he dead, too? He was sure Sam could help and that sister of his, with her "telepathic nonsense", as Sam had called it – surely she could help answer some of the questions, too.

He arrived at the station, about two miles from where Sam and his family lived, just after twelve o'clock. He glanced round aimlessly, until he spotted the taxi rank. He hoped it wouldn't be too much. He'd brought some money of his own and a few pounds his aunt had given him, but factory workers didn't get much of a wage, just enough to get him by, week by week. Most of his money went on helping his aunt with bills. His indulgence was buying a couple of singles each week or saving up for an LP. The local newsagent's had a box of old singles that you could riffle through until you found one that brought back a few entertaining memories or that you missed when it was in the charts. There was a certain pleasure in finding a record that you had really liked and taking it home to play over and over. His musings distracted him momentarily and gave some brief pleasure to what had become a crowded and explosive train of thought.

He knocked gingerly on his arrival. Sam answered almost immediately and ushered him upstairs. His mother was still in bed and Rosie was sitting with her own thoughts in her own room.

"How are you?" As soon as he had spoken the words he faltered, embarrassed how could anyone be feeling, having just found out their mother had been murdered! But he was avoiding the next truth he knew had to be spoken aloud, afraid to break the reticent stillness with the heinous words that his father was the suspected murderer of his mother.

The deafening silence lingered for just seconds but penetrated the room in a weighty, black form, which did not intend to disperse for some time. Paul laid his blue Adidas bag down in front of Sam's stereo and automatically sifted through the records next to it, linking the remnants of his previous thoughts to the room he had now been placed in. Before either spoke again, Rosie stood at the threshold of the bedroom and interrupted the silence. "Hi." Paul had met her before a couple of times in London but was not expecting to enjoy the sudden pleasure of such a beauty on what was becoming a rather dismal afternoon. He couldn't help himself and smiled invitingly at Sam's sister. Slightly disarmed, Rosie smiled back. He was obviously a charmer and she found herself immediately liking those dark, admiring eyes. This brief encounter distracted both the boys from the alarming words that Sam suddenly announced:

"They think my father killed her."

Paul did not speak for a moment, digesting the words like an unpleasant mouthful of overspiced food.

"He didn't do it," Rosie affirmed. Acknowledging the meaning suddenly, Paul turned sharply to Sam.

"Your dad?"

"Yes. They've arrested him for her murder." The shocking bluntness was easy between friends who had shared many controversial and damning conversations in the past. Rosie attempted a more helpful dialogue:

"My parents were there at the time of the murder and my father was alone in the villa when they think she was murdered. But he didn't do it." The defiant calmness in her voice was convincing. Paul was lingering on those simple facts, which pointed the finger securely at their father, but he was thinking of someone else completely.

"I think it was her husband…Gavin."

Rosie sat thoughtfully on the edge of the bed. "Is he tall, dark eyes, a bit like my dad's, rather sophisticated-looking," she mused, "with a sports car?"

"Yes, that's him," Paul hissed, surprised at how accurate her description was and realising that in fact that was basically all he knew.

"I've seen him." Her remark was defined with a sense of alarm.

"When? I haven't seen him since before my mum disappeared. I thought he might be dead, too."

"No, I mean I've 'seen' him."

Paul's look of confusion was to be expected, Sam thought. He hadn't grown up with his sister's 'all-knowing eye'! Sam had several unsavoury terms for her senses, irritated by her on many occasions but also accepting of her ways. He saw the whole 'package' and he loved her eccentricities really. There was nothing malicious about her and she had looked after him enough over the years. He suddenly couldn't think of anyone he would rather have around right now, even his mate Paul. Sam simply encouraged her, while Paul looked on quizzically and with an obvious scepticism, although he was clearly aware of what she meant, from the stories Sam had told him, in one of many confidential conversations about family.

She began to verbalise the shaky visons forming like a mist clearing, to project a firm, clear image like unedited scenes from a film. The man she saw, climbing out of his car, was following someone: you could tell from his furtive behaviour and she sensed his threatening, jealous manner. He was in the city one moment and then on some bleak, dusty road the next. She was sure this was Italy but there was no beautiful Tuscan villa in her mind. And then she 'saw' him on some idyllic beach, smoothing the hair of a woman with long, blonde hair, which was like a scene from a completely different film, inserted randomly and out of place. He looked a lot older in that image, suggesting it might be a 'vision', placed firmly in the present. And then the scenes moved abruptly to the one which had become much more familiar to her, the one of her father, in a cell, haggard, exhausted from all the questions, confused and crying quietly in his own scrambled thoughts.

Rosie felt her own tears on her wet cheek and automatically wiped them away. The boys looked at her, engrossed in her 'story'. "There's a police officer, Gina something, and I think she might be able to help," she finally blurted out. The Three Amigos, Sam thought as a rather childish response, caught up in the bond that had suddenly emerged, relieving the desperate tension of this dramatic and serious situation.

"The one with the inspector?"

"Yes."

"I met her, too. They're the ones who came to our house," Paul interjected.

The animated conversation had disturbed Marjorie. Until now she hadn't the energy to move, to venture out of the bedroom. She had worked out that the visitor was Sam's friend, Paul and that they were talking about the death… about Jim. Until now she didn't want to get involved with their incessant mutterings which only made her feel that the world was conspiring to ruin her family and any chance of happiness; to destroy her marriage and her life. Her tears still flowed in an endless stream, but were now deadened by an emotional blackout. But the tone had changed with a gentle lilt of hope that made her reach for her dressing gown and wistfully wander towards her son's bedroom, to the door left ajar as if offering a way in. She was momentarily disturbed by the thought that this was like the scene she had studied from *Macbeth*: his arrival at the witches' coven. As she hovered, awaiting the premonitions that would lead to her final downfall, Rosie's voice lifted her up briefly, securing her thoughts with the living and with hope.

"Are you okay, Mum?" Her voice was like a soothing promise of goodness and peace, and she moved forward with a strange emptiness and asked, "Would you like something to eat?" The mundane question was holding her firm, grounding her in reality; it came as a welcome diversion to their conspiracy.

They sat around the breakfast table, Rosie and her mother picking at the cheese and pickle sandwiches, watching the two boys devouring theirs, saying very little except polite necessities, until Marjorie automatically started clearing up, cleaning the dishes in a sinister, robotic stance.

"Let me help," Paul offered. Standing beside her, he was reminded of his aunt and leant over to touch her hand.

"It will be alright," he assured her, thoughtfully. His genuine support encouraged a smile, something her children hadn't seen for a while. Sam had been surprised by how calm Paul had been. There had been no blame, no angry or threatening accusations. He assumed most of this was because of his hate for Gavin and the fact that for a long time his mother had not been a part of his life. He also hoped their friendship was important to him.

Rosie, Sam and Paul decided to go for a walk shortly after lunch; Marjorie had gone for a lie-down. Paul sat perched on the stair and pulled on his trainers. A small thread was hanging from the back and he contemplated their shabbiness. "When did they get this worn?" The Birches had a really nice home and the shoes he was looking at underneath the telephone table, were fashionable and new. He was suddenly envious. He remembered buying his trainers with his aunt at least a year ago, before all this, before he knew about his mother's death, before... He visualised a rotting corpse, his mother's hair mangled with mud and worms – wriggling, slimy worms – crawling. He tried to stop, blinking, painfully trying to diffuse the gruesome images that invaded his mind.

"Are you okay?" Rosie laid her hand gently on his arm. He was brought back to the comforting reality of his surroundings and was grateful.

"Remember her before. Remember her hug, her smile, the precious moments you had with her." He tried but they were too few, too long ago. "Your aunt then." She seemed to read his mind. Rosie was aware of the strength of her perception at that moment. Her empathetic responses came easily. She looked at Paul with a keenness that startled her. She liked him. She really liked him, unexpectedly realising there had been an instant attraction. She was sure he felt it, too.

The clouds had gathered, blocking out the sun, but they were not threatening and offered some hope as the blueness and warmth of the sky attempted to break through overhead. Paul was reluctant to speak, despite his nagging wish to find answers to the questions that bothered him. As the clouds weakened, giving in to the brightness of the sun, his confidence strengthened.

"I need to know why my mother would rush off to Tuscany to the villa where your parents were staying." Rosie had her suspicions but ones that she was not allowing herself to consider. To them it was a random coincidence. Her father had the answers, she was sure, but the answers were hiding silently and Paul had learnt nothing from his visit, except that he did not believe Sam and Rosie's father was guilty either. He'd also learnt how much this family meant to him and he was saddened by his decision to return to London the next day, back to his aunt. There was nothing much he could do. His main priority now was to get another job. He needed to get on with his life. He also had an additional wish now; he hoped his future would include his friendship, not only with Sam, but with Rosie, too.

CHAPTER 7

Gina leant thoughtfully on the palm of her hand, idly gazing again at the file in front of her. With no other leads, Jim Birch was about to be charged with Lucy Jameson's murder. She was uncomfortable. It didn't seem right and there were so many missing leads because of the problems coordinating information with the Italian Police. She had several other cases pending now. Her status in the office had been given a boost by the Birch case. Her intelligence and creativity of thought was being developed at last. While she pondered over the last few scribbles she had written, distracted from the hit-and-run case she should have been focused on, the telephone rang. It was the front desk.

"Jim Birch's daughter is here. She wonders if she can speak to you." There was a suggestion of coincidence, as her notes on the Birch family stared back at her, intriguing Gina, as she welcomed the young woman into her office.

When Rosie's ramblings ceased, she expected the police officer to either laugh, dismiss her or seek advice from a shrink! She was well aware of how she sounded, like a freak or beloved daughter desperately trying to divert the attention towards another suspect and away from her father, but instead she was surprised to see the officer lean forward with a querulous look of interest.

"What did you say this man's name was? Her husband's name?"

"Gavin, Gavin Jameson."

"But we have no record of a Mr Gavin Jameson. The name in her passport was Lucy Jameson but there is no record of a marriage." Gina was aware that this last detail she had spoken aloud was what had been bothering her all along; an important detail, passed over without consideration in the hasty search for evidence which would back up their theory that Jim Birch killed her. There was evidence and statements concerning his affair years ago with the woman and Paul was very likely his son, but there was very little about Lucy's boyfriend at the time. And how did she have a passport with a new married name if there was no evidence of a marriage? There had only been a brief effort to try to trace him, without any success. For Gina, there were far too many unanswered questions.

Gina decided to ignore the fact that this young lady seemed to have strange, unexplained psychic visions; she'd come across similar types before. With the fact that Rosie was so convincing and the fact she also desperately wanted to find another suspect for the murder, apart from Jim Birch, she wrote down as many details as she could, planning to spend her weekend on the case, before they charged Birch and sent down the wrong man.

The first avenue of enquiry came from the addresses, telephone numbers and other details she had been given via their friend Paul. She was well aware of the bizarre coincidence that linked them to the case, but they were obviously unaware of such a bond and it was best it was left that way for now.

The details written down were as suspected: bogus. She couldn't understand how this woman had been so easily fooled. There was definitely no marriage recorded: she had checked thoroughly. It was assumed that she had changed her name as some sort of disguise or new start. She had been spotted walking along the lane which led to the Tuscan villa in question but she had been alone. Studying the details further she was aware that there were no questions asked about other strangers in the area at that time. Annoyed by her own failings, she began to make telephone calls to the local police and surrounding places that might have some recollection of another stranger at that time. A male. It was a long time ago and a long shot, but it was worth a try.

Saturday afternoon she spent looking through files, documents and clippings; checking databases and asking questions, searching old records of flights and hotels, apartments in the vicinity...trying to 'find' this mysterious Gavin Jameson. That evening she was interrupted by a call from Italy.

"Is that Miss Gina Russo?" the voice enquired. Rosemary spoke with a quiet nervousness. "This is Rosemary – from the villa in Tuscany. You gave me your number in case I heard or thought of anything." Gina couldn't help but think someone was up there, smiling down on her and offering support in this case. This was the second time in two days she'd been involved in unexpected conversations which might help her.

"Yes, this is Gina. Thank you for ringing." They conversed with a serious politeness but there was an obvious empathic link between them. Rosemary had stumbled upon some information when talking casually to one of the locals the previous morning. Mrs Bianchi was a generous neighbour and full of kindness, although she loved to natter. Like many Italians, her ability to talk tirelessly, with engaging stories and helpful advice, led back to the murder at Rosemary's villa. It was a wonderful, exciting narrative to explore with concern and passionate affection. Mrs Bianchi mentioned the sports car that had been parked down her lane, about half an hour's walk from Rosemary's property. Did she think it had belonged to the woman who was murdered? She told her she had looked out hoping to see a dark, handsome man with it, to whisk her away from her husband and four children, laughing at her own amusing idea. She was disappointed when she heard the engine roar to life and missed the owner. Despite rushing to the upstairs window, where she could get a good look, she saw only the flash of the back bumper and number plate as it sped away. Rosemary was sure no one had mentioned a sports car and she assumed the police must know about it, but she had decided to ring Gina anyway. Penny had been in constant contact with Rosemary, desperate to help her in-laws, and on several occasions had used the words, "Any leads might help". This was exactly what Gina needed. No car had been mentioned or known about. This was enough to cause reasonable doubt for Jim Birch's conviction. She rang Ian immediately.

"I've got a lead on the Tuscan murder case," she told him, the excitement evident as she delivered the words.

CHAPTER 8

Jim was exhausted by all the questioning. He had had plenty of time to sit and think. However hard he tried, he could remember very little about that afternoon. He was beginning to think he might have had some sort of blackout or seizure in the heat and killed her after all! He didn't really feel that was plausible, though. Now that he knew the body belonged to the Lucy who had worked in his office, the woman he had had an affair with, he felt guilty of her death, whether he had killed her or not. The part of this horrible nightmare that triggered most fear and alarm, however, was the child. She had a son. Considering his age and the likeness – those dark brown eyes – he could well be the father. And he knew him. He'd liked Sam's friend in London, his mum liked him, his wife liked him! What a mess. The irony was almost laughable. He was getting what he deserved. He felt like a cad – he was a cad. He had no idea how this would end. At that moment the cell felt like a haven, but prison? He wasn't sure his actions deserved that harsh a punishment. His head throbbed. The guilt was suffocating and the tears came again, merging with the incessant, throbbing sobs.

The door rattled and an echoing clang signalled the door opening. Wiping the tears away, embarrassed by his vulnerability, he looked at the woman entering his confined space. He recognised the policewoman and involuntarily let out a deep sigh as he prepared for more questioning; questions he did not have the answers to.

Her smile was disconcerting. The unexpected warmth she was exhibiting provided a sudden sense of hope.

"You have been given bail. You are still a prime suspect in this case, but we are exploring new evidence at the moment and you can return home while the investigations proceed. You will be expected to cooperate with further questioning, but you can go home." She was succinct in her speech, but the warmth was still there. The tears came again but this time softly with the relief he was beginning to feel.

"Your wife is waiting for you," she added. An unsettling panic returned as he knew he had to face his family and friends with the awful truths that had been divulged in the last two weeks. Marjorie ran forward to meet her husband as he was led through the heavy glass door into the corridor where she had been waiting. There was no need for words. They would come later. He was coming home.

The journey home was quiet. There was an awkward silence between them, interrupted by soft smiles. Marjorie found the strength and broke the silence.

"Was it Lucy from the office? Did you kill her?" It was

such an abrupt question but her need for an answer which had been building up over the past few days made it impossible for her to control the outburst.

"Yes, it was her, but no, I didn't kill her." Jim was not angered by her question, in fact he felt a relief in being able to state such words firmly and confirm his denial to himself as well as his wife. Marjorie smiled more openly and laid her hand on his knee.

"I love you."

"I love you, too."

As she parked the car on the drive, Jim leant towards her and embraced her firmly, giving him the confidence to speak with determination.

"I need to tell the children."

"Later. Let's just enjoy this evening together."

Jim panicked briefly, as he stood on the threshold of his own home. He felt like an intruder, a criminal, wary. Rosie and Sam rushed forward and hugged him and his anxiety subsided, replaced with guilt and more silent tears. He looked at Rosie for some guidance, some support as his emotions strangled him.

"It's okay dad, you can cry if you like. It's been horrible for you." And he fell into the nearest chair and sobbed. Sam rallied round with the cups of tea and carried his dad's things upstairs, pausing on the landing to wipe away a few tears of his own.

"Right, Sam's run you a bath and then we are going for a

walk before tea. I only want happy talk." Marjorie's orders gathered them up decisively with a sense of purpose which defined and relaxed the tension surrounding them. She knew he'd want some time to himself, some time to settle.

When Jim finally came downstairs and joined them in the lounge, he looked much more relaxed, less grubby and more like himself.

"Shall we go, then?" he asked cheerily. They walked out along the path leading to fields at the back of a large, pink Georgian house. The weeds and thistles had been stamped down to provide an easy walkway. Two small children ran ahead with their mother, but other than their delighted squeals, it was deserted and peaceful. Walking with a comfortable stride, Rosie talked about her studies and Sam described an edited version of his latest antics at the local park with some mates Marjorie told some school stories, keeping the conversation light. There were several quiet, contemplative pauses as they enjoyed each other's company and the natural surroundings which brought with them their own relaxing relief.

The large oak tree, a focal point ahead, stretched out its twisted limbs, offering the open space as a peaceful haven. The magpies danced playfully amongst the grasses and bushes around the edge of the field. Two settled just in front of them.

"Two for joy," Rosie murmured just before they flew off, joined further up on the bank by another two magpies.

"Four for a boy," she thought, keeping the words safely in her head as she thought of Paul.

After Paul had left, just a few days later, her mother had busied herself around the house with a nervous energy. She was taking more care of herself and she had a determined manner as she began to take control. It was on the Thursday evening after tea that she had summoned her and her brother to the lounge. She wanted to talk to them. Marjorie had wanted to talk to the children about her father, about secrets from their past that were now very much part of their future. She was well aware that Paul might be Jim's son. She wasn't stupid! Sam and Rosie sat expectantly on the sofa, waiting to hear the story their mother insisted needed to be told.

"It was just a brief affair," she concluded, "and I forgave him, but that's the reason the police think your father was involved in her murder." She waited for the children to respond. The silence, though brief, seemed to grow, consuming them. Rosie's mind was leaping wildly. Paul. She knew there was something. She thought her feelings were of a romantic nature, but she now realised what she had felt could be some sort of sisterly bond.

"Could Paul be dad's son?" Her mother was not alarmed. It had been a thought regularly playing on her mind. "Yes, I think he might be." She had paled slightly. Saying the words was more powerful than thinking them.

Sam's fixed stare spoke the words he could not utter. He got up suddenly, stormed out of the room, and they heard the front door bang behind him.

"Don't worry, Mum. It's quite a shock. You know Sam, he'll disappear for a bit but he'll be back." The two women sat for a moment holding hands.

"I'll make a cup of tea." Rosie got up and ventured into the kitchen, needing her own space, needing to work through her own tumultuous feelings and thoughts. Marjorie sat alone, glancing towards the door from which Rosie had disappeared, and curling her feet up and hugging her knees. Marjorie sighed heavily, releasing the tension and emotions that had been building up for weeks. "Now to pick up the pieces," she thought.

Rosie and her mother had become soulmates during her father's absence. Penny and John had avoided them recently, not because they weren't caring or felt anything different than supportive love for them all, it was just that they didn't know what to say or do to help. Their awkwardness was harder to deal with than their absence. John was dealing with the solicitors for his brother and wrote a really sensitive and generous letter to him, but staying away helped them both. Neither of them knew what to say face to face. When Marjorie rang Penny that evening about Sam going missing again, she was straight round. Their concerns for Sam alleviated their more pressing concerns for Jim. It provided a strange relief from the horrific reality of the murder and Jim's involvement.

There had been outbursts of anger and mornings when Sam would just sleep in and not get out of bed until after midday. They knew he was smoking pot again which precipitated his mood swings – but they couldn't blame him. Rosie's nagging fears for Sam continued to disturb her.

"You must stop worrying about your brother. You've always worried about him, since you were very young. It will make you ill. You cannot live his life." Her Auntie Penny's words resounded in her brain. Her mother had not allowed herself to worry anymore. It wore her out.

Marjorie had collapsed on the kitchen stool after one of his moods.

"I just want your dad home," she had cried.

Sam strode purposefully and wilfully forward, watching the pavement move like an escalator beneath his feet. He barely looked up, absorbing himself in the varying browns of abandoned broken twigs and tree debris, avoiding contact with his thoughts. Listening briefly to the chirruping birds busy living their short lives, he moved steadily on, fighting back the welling tears. He increased his pace, breaking into a run, propelled by an urge to get away. It was at least five minutes later, before he stopped to regain his senses. Walking off, running away, that was his way of coping. He was thinking suddenly of his jaunt to London in Terry's car. His family had been worried sick, but then he felt carefree, just a child, worrying about no one or anything; now he felt a weight of responsibility and confusion, of a needy family falling apart and he felt totally lost. He had no idea who to turn to. A wall had been constructed around Paul, his own doing, but threatening and unstable. Remembering his 'trip' to London with Terry and Paul, he thought smoking pot would be a good idea right now. He believed alcohol was the more evil temptation; his behaviour became erratic and sometimes violent. Alcohol always brought out an obnoxious side to him that instigated trouble. A smoke was calming, chilling, and he could lose himself softly and quietly with his friends. He hadn't seen Nick or Tony for a while, but he knew where to find them.

CHAPTER 9

Gina's attention had not been on her cases or the menial tasks she was required to administer in the office. She was making mistakes. When she was called into the inspector's office, she knew Ian was going to reprimand her; she was risking losing her promotion, or even worse her job.

"I think you should take a holiday." If it wasn't for the kind eyes and suggestion of a smile, she would have thought it was a precursor for a dismissal or move down the ranks.

"How about a trip to Italy?" he suggested. He was well aware of his prodigy's continued unauthorised work on the Birch case and this new, though rather tenuous, lead was worthy of following up. Until this case was solved properly, he knew he could not rely on Gina to focus in her usual judicious manner on any of the other files pending. He thought she might consider talking to the Birch family about taking the rather curious daughter with her. He was in agreement with the majority of humankind: he didn't believe in any of that mumbo-jumbo psychic stuff, but she certainly had an eye for detail and perhaps she knew more than she had let on; something she heard when she was young or a photograph or something from the earliest recesses of her memory. Steve was not bothered about how or what she knew, but if she could help, fine.

Penny agreed to go with Rosie. Marjorie didn't like the thought of her travelling alone, and Penny and John were in total agreement. John was notably concerned about her travelling with a police officer, however kind and sincere she seemed. John would stay around, keep an eye on Marjorie, Jim and Sam and let his wife enjoy some time with her niece. Sam was acting odd, being overly helpful, and the ideal son one minute and then storming off in a violent rage the next. When Sam blurted out that he was thinking of going to stay with Paul for a while, there was an obvious concern.

"He did say I could stay anytime," he added. Although Paul had been unsettled by the knowledge that they might be brothers, that Rosie might be his sister and that he had a real father – he liked them. He had kept his distance, quite aware of Sam's offhand attitude. Sam was weak, he thought. They had been close friends when they were younger but now his childish, impetuous behaviour irritated him. When he'd called last week, he seemed changed. He had grown up, and his offer to let him stay was genuine. Sam needed him, just like he had needed Sam just a few months before. His aunt knew nothing about Sam's dad and his mother. She had not been told. She would never accept Jim, the man who had broken her sister's heart and caused her to marry a man whom she now thought of as a murderer, too. She blamed herself for all of it.

Marjorie sensed her loss again immediately. They were just beginning to rebuild their lives as a family and now Rosie and Paul were going away. Jim was more understanding.

"We all have our own way of dealing with things." His words were loaded. Besides, he wanted time alone with his wife, despite his love for his children. Jim and Marjorie were like newly-weds, conscious of each other's feelings all the time, wanting to stay together, holding hands, not saying much but rekindling their marriage. Leaving them alone for a few days would be helpful. Besides, John and Penny were often travelling around with business or on what they considered to be 'well-deserved breaks'. Tuscany remained a favourite haunt of theirs.

CHAPTER 10

Allen turned to Rosemary as they sat on the patio enjoying a second glass of Chianti.

"I know you love this place, Rosemary, but it is not the same anymore since..." He trailed off, not wanting to address the events that had corrupted her idyllic world and their peace.

"I think we should sell up and move back to England or at least find another place...somewhere else." It was evident from his pause that he did not want to upset his wife further. Rosemary was looking thoughtfully at this kind man, her dear husband. He was looking tired, old even. At 72 he might be considered old, but he had changed in just over a year from a spritely businessman full of sexy energy, clever and busy, to someone weary and dishevelled, weighed down with life. She hadn't noticed the transformation until now, her mind occupied with her own problems. Money was not part of their worries because of his competence, despite everything, but the impact of the murder investigation had taken its toll.

"What about Dad?"

"We wouldn't be moving straight away. It will take time

to sell and move on." Rosemary nodded, understanding the significance of what he said. Her father's heart was weak. He had had two minor strokes, probably brought on by the events of the past year. Stanley was quite aware he was living on borrowed time, even though neither of them had mentioned it.

"I'll think about it," was her simple repost. She did not wish to leave Italy. She did not want to leave her dream home, forced out by events that were out of her control, but she was well aware of the impact this whole terrible business had had on her husband.

When Penny rang, asking if she could accept visitors at such short notice, she immediately said, "Yes!" It would be a helpful distraction and she could cogitate her thoughts with her friend. Rosie had established quite a name for herself with friends and family with her uncanny foresight. Apparently, she had heard that this 'sight' had run in the family. She might be able to offer some guidance, too. She was not very happy about the fact that they were coming with a police officer; however, she had liked the policewoman who was half-Italian, and if she could help her friend then she couldn't see any harm in their visit. Too much harm had been done already. Rosemary was well into her sixties now but, like her husband, she had always seemed a lot younger. As she looked out through the large window, across the Tuscan valley, she felt at ease. Nothing could bother her now. The damage had been done and they were almost back to normal. Any further inconveniences would not drive her away. She walked back out onto the patio, where Allen was sipping his wine and contemplating the view. Their conversation was brief as always, and as always, he agreed to whatever made his wife happy.

"Are you okay, then, with the visit?"

"Not really, but if it's what you want, then it's what I want." An answer she was familiar with in their comfortable and consistent marriage together.

"I might go back to London, though, while they are here, tie up a few loose ends and look at some options, should we decide to leave here."

"I want to stay," she replied steadily as she took in the view, drawing it in, implanting the beautiful vision into her memory – just in case. Allen nodded but said nothing. There was no need.

Rosemary welcomed her guests in her usual hospitable manner. She hadn't realised just how much she had missed Penny. Her father, Stanley, would sit quietly these days, on his own, in the self-sufficient annex they had built for him. He slept much of the time and wandered around muttering nonsense, but he seemed happy. Although he had trouble walking these days, ate little and communicated even less, he ventured out to greet them. He seemed to brighten at the sight of Penny. The young girl with them engaged his interest, too. Her dark hair was pulled up into a ponytail, her sunglasses hiding her eyes. He was glad he had made the special effort to get up, shave and put on his best trousers and shirt.

Rosie was the first to step forward and she gave him a huge hug. "Hello, Stanley," she beamed, giving him a welcoming squeeze. "It's so lovely to see you again." He was rather overcome by this obvious shower of affection but his heart opened up to this lovely young lady immediately, delighted by the embrace. He didn't remember her, but they had only met once in England, when he had travelled over to England with Rosemary, and stayed with Penny and John. They had a lovely home and he had enjoyed their short visit immensely, even if now he was struggling to remember any details. Rosie suddenly missed her grandparents very much, the image of her own Grandad Stanley keen in her mind. This frail man was also near "his time", and suddenly death seemed all around her. The rest of the group watched her rather indulgent outburst. Such indulgent outbursts of affection were rare in this villa, but Rosie often took people by surprise and this occasion was no exception. The sunny and loving mood she created was welcomed, particularly here and now, when the purpose of the visit hung heavily like a black cloud. Gina admired her captivating liveliness. She only had admiration and attraction for this young woman and it continued to flourish; a friendship that would develop long after this case was concluded.

Rosie had been given the room her parents had stayed in. She was sure this had been arranged intentionally, hoping it might help her see more clearly, work out what happened and clear her father of this awful crime. The compact, wooden stairs led up to a door which opened to her room. It was quite large, the generous bed centred majestically below one of the shuttered windows, its impressive dark wood ornated with sculptured flowers and leaves. A white crocheted cover made it homely; the white sheets crisp and clean, fresh and cool. Though quite sparse, the heavy dressing table filled the room comfortably, offering a few home comforts: a small, colourful pottery dish, filled with perfumed soaps, and two freshly laundered, fluffy towels, folded neatly next to a matching hairbrush and mirror. It reminded her of her grandmother's set, temporarily. A delicate lamp, with a glass stand, was carefully arranged on a small metal bedside table, covered with a crocheted mat, matching the bedspread.

There were two windows. One was open slightly, looking out onto a small tiled courtyard, decorated with pots and plants and a wooden bench, painted in yellow and green, to match the backdrop that framed the scene. She pushed the wooden slats gently, to reveal more of the view. Beyond the courtyard, she could see the Tuscan hills stretched out; undulating greens of various hues, dotted with the occasional suggestion of a building or row of trees. The window over the bed was screened by the shutters, pulled closed and clipped with a small hook, keeping the room cool and the midges outside. Opening this window, anticipating a different view, she was pleasantly rewarded with the sight of the glistening pool below, shimmering and winking in the sunlight. Captivated by the beauty of her surroundings, she leant on the sill and dreamily immersed herself in its pleasure.

Rosie unpacked her things, holding up the new swimsuit her Auntie Penny had treated her to, admiring the vivacious colours. She placed it neatly with her other clothes, in the empty drawers, before venturing downstairs to the further delights the villa had to offer and to her hosts.

The coals on the barbeque hissed as the steaks and sausages were turned and the Chianti continued to flow. Rosie kept to the fresh orange juice she had been offered. She did not wish to cloud her visions or disrupt her thoughts; she did not want anything to spoil her chances of finding out what had happened. Gina retired to bed and to a book she was reading, shortly after supper, leaving the family and friends alone, enjoying their reunion.

In the morning they slept in, having relished too much wine. Except for the policewoman, Gina, the other women gathered by the pool after a leisurely breakfast of bread and varying jams and fruit. They were dressed lightly in their costumes ready to delight in the heat of the sun and the coolness of the water, which glistened magically against the bewitching beauty of the Tuscan valley. Gina had gone out. She was keen to investigate the sightings and stories that had recently come to light. This was Rosie's first time abroad. She lay back, absorbing the sun's torrid rays. Her body reddened, reacting angrily to the unfamiliar blistering heat. Her Auntie Penny had no problem adjusting, her browning skin, subtly recognising such conditions, accustomed to sunny holidays abroad. She tossed a bottle to Rosie.

"Here, put this cream on or you'll burn." Rosie dutifully followed her instructions, enjoying the cool, silky sensation as she massaged it in, easing the dryness of her skin. They allowed themselves to savour the pleasures of their surroundings, involved in idle chatter or quietly reflecting on their lives, intermittently dozing and sipping the drinks provided on the small, wooden tray. Rosemary talked about the locals, and her anecdotes of visitors from over the years, allowing the three of them to indulge in laughter and warm smiles, bonding like old friends.

Rosie got up, feeling relaxed and at ease and wandered around the pool aimlessly. Becoming more aware of the inner peace she was feeling, she began to open up her mind. She seemed to be waiting and watching. She was now walking back towards the pool, having undertaken an amble along the path which meandered around the garden. The belief that she would learn something from this visit to Italy was strong. Without realising, she had stopped by a sunbed, resting her hand on an old marble ledge that had once housed a statue and now supported a ricotta pot and blossoming plant, seductively drawing your eye to its colourful beauty. Her hand burned. It was here. The image came swiftly, moving like a hawk from the sky, plummeting towards her.

The vision was so clear. The young, blonde woman was watching Jim from the sporadic bushes, hidden from view, quietly staring. Jim was dozing. Rosie watched the images unravelling: the woman moving forward, appearing from some bushes, planting something in her father's water. Rosie was watching her, watching her father and then she saw him murder her.

CHAPTER 11

Lucy's son's friend Terry had boasted about his brother who was dealing drugs. She had liked the boy initially, but now she had concerns about his friendship with her son. She banned him from coming round to the house when she realised he was from the estate and from an unsavoury family. But lately she was hardly around. She was not there to keep an eye on him. She spotted Terry's brother hanging around once, looking furtive and that's when he had offered the drug. "In case you need to keep a check on that boyfriend of yours," he had said. She was irritated at the time, but after the wedding she felt an anxious fear in her husband's presence, and late one afternoon she caught up with him and impulsively accepted his offering. She kept it in her handbag, 'just in case', although she wasn't sure why. She knew Terry's brother was bad news, but he had been very helpful when she had approached him. He wasn't interested in what she had to say. He was very interested in the money, though, always looking for a deal. Money ruled his life. He did not intend to hang around this area of London long. As soon as he could obtain a sufficient stash, he would be off. He told her the tablet was really effective.

Her husband would know nothing about what happened to him, while he was under its influence. He would have a terrible headache in the morning but he would not remember anything that had happened. She could do what she liked to her 'victim'. His sneer was ugly. How could the little boy Terry that played so nicely with her son, have such an unpleasant family? The person in front of her was barely a man himself, probably only fourteen or fifteen, but his path was one of crime and hate. She hoped Terry would not end up the same way and felt suddenly guilty that she had sent him packing last time he was at the house. His brother smiled and stashed the money in his back pocket, swaggering away as if he owned the street. He enjoyed the thought of this woman getting her own back on some sleazy guy, his thoughts unsavoury and mean.

Lucy had not been thinking about her husband as she fingered the pill in its plastic casing. Her thoughts had been passionate, desperate, incensed with a deep love. The drug would enable her to lie with him, be with him, indulging in her fantasies. When she had the courage, she would talk to him. It was sort of a plan. She was acting on instinct. There was no sense in any of this.

And now she was here. She knew they had all gone out. It was steadily silent. Standing momentarily by the statue, she found the meagre tablet in the small pocket of her bag. She clutched it nervously, her hand sweating in the heat. He didn't see her walking lightly over to the water, depositing the drug into his glass and moving back out of sight. He was in a deep sleep, soaking up the heat. She stood, hidden amongst the newly dug earth and plants… waiting.

Jim was sitting on the edge of the sunbed now, he looked confused and tired.

"Jim," she called softly. He looked up, registering her. She moved swiftly to embrace him, kissing him tenderly on the lips and then with more passion. He responded, breathing heavily.

"Oh, Jim. I love you. I've always loved you," her hot breath in his hair. There was a sudden disturbance behind her and she turned instinctively.

"Gavin!" The shock was instant. She let Jim go, just as her husband rushed over, grabbing her hair and pulling her to her feet. His hands gripped her neck in a frenzied, angry impulse, squeezing tighter and tighter, until her body slumped like a rag doll and fell limp and lifeless to the ground. Jim was in some sort of drugged stupor, unconscious almost and unknowing. Gavin dragged her body back towards the bushes and that's where he buried her.

Rosemary heard the cry first. It was like the wail of a wounded animal. Rosie lay crumpled on the hard concrete, splattered by pieces of a broken terracotta pot and sprawling plant mingled with earth.

"Oh my God! Rosie!" Penny leapt off the chair she had

been sitting idly on just a moment ago and rushed over, followed by Rosemary. Rosie looked bemused, her head throbbing.

"I'm okay," she managed shakily.

"Whatever happened?"

"I think I fainted. It must have been the heat." She was reluctant to divulge the real reason; the images she had seen. It was all rather unbelievable, a wild dream, and yet she knew she should tell Gina, however absurd.

"I think I'll go and lie down for a bit." Penny and Rosemary fussed over her until she was settled in the cool room, the fan purring above her. The glass of water beside her upset her briefly as the image of her father and the blonde woman came into view. When they had left her to rest and sleep, she wrote down the thoughts palpitating with a troublesome determination, before she could close her eyes and slip into a restless sleep.

When Gina returned, Penny and Rosemary invited her to join them on the patio to enjoy the late-afternoon sun, as it filtered its crimson-red and deep orange rays across the horizon. Enjoying a glass of wine with her companions, they told her about the morning's drama. Penny suspected she had had one of her 'visions'. Although she was familiar with these perceptive interruptions, having talked to Rosie as a trustworthy companion as well as aunt, for much of her life, this time had been different, more intense, and she had been alarmed by its impact on her.

"It must have been quite forceful and unpleasant, to make her faint like that." She was well aware of her niece's fit-like encounters. Although they were infrequent, they had been influential in their lives. Penny spoke openly to Gina and Rosemary, confiding tales from the past. Their short time together had already established a confidence between them. Rosemary was engrossed by these anecdotes of strange coincidences, leaning forward, captivated by Penny's words, like a nosey neighbour. Life was rarely this interesting or dramatic for her, in this small village in Tuscany, "That is until you have a murder in your back garden!" she thought to herself. Gina was more composed in her reactions. Obviously sceptic, she could not help being caught up in Penny's storytelling. Such coincidences rarely happen with such regularity and indisputable influence, although coincidences are what they were. What she had learnt that afternoon from the local neighbour, supported what Rosie had said and she was hoping Rosie might be able to divulge more helpful clues, notably now there was a possibility she had seemingly 'seen' something this afternoon. She wanted very much at that moment to check on Rosie, although she realised it was more out of curiosity than real concern. Gina excused herself, suggesting she might 'pop in' and see how the 'patient' was feeling.

"Good idea, she's been asleep for a while and I've got a feeling she'd rather talk to you about what happened than to us," Penny contemplated, feeling somewhat put out by this fact, as she spoke it aloud. She understood, with a degree of generosity, that as her aunt and not her mother, there were times when she needed to step back and not interfere.

Gina tapped gently on the door of Rosie's room. She could hear her moving about.

"Just a minute!" Rosie opened the door dressed in a robe similar to the one that hung on her bathroom door. She was not surprised to see her visitor, but avoiding any direct questions, said, "Come and look at this view."

She beckoned Gina over.

"I have a similar view, but you can't quite see the bench. There's more of the front path on the other side. Beautiful, isn't it?"

The idle exchange relaxed them into an amiable conversation, allowing Rosie to move easily into the more pressing revelations.

"Shall we go and sit on that bench? It provides some shade and it might be more pleasurable to talk there," Gina suggested.

Rosie nodded and smiled, following her back down the stairs and outside, acquiring two glasses of water from the kitchen on their way out. Rosemary had encouraged her guests to help themselves to anything in the fridge or kitchen.

They sat quietly for a few minutes, sipping the water, Gina waiting patiently for her young companion to speak first, despite her sense of urgency and anticipation. Rosie's silent tears trickled softly down her cheeks as she spoke; the occasional droplet left a dark ring on the thin cotton shawl she had draped over her shoulders. And Gina listened. The uncanny details drew a vivid picture in her mind. It seemed to be just a story, a good plot for a novel, but the reality of the place, the characters and from the information she had acquired that afternoon, clarified her understanding of the events that happened all those years ago. There was no proof. There was no one who would believe her. Although the old woman had confirmed the sightings, the young, blonde English woman, followed shortly after by the sports car: she had not seen the man. It was enough for Gina, however, to continue her search for the missing Gavin Jameson and make him the main suspect in Lucy's murder case. Rosie felt exhausted. Even though the police were unlikely to believe her fantastical story, she knew in her mind that her father was innocent. It was enough for her family, for her. She knew her father had not murdered this young woman. And Gina, she was sure, knew it, too.

Over the next couple of days Gina came and went, following leads, spending much of her time being persistent and irritating the local police and locals. The rest of them, enjoyed Rosemary's hospitality, the mood light, airy and relaxed. Stanley's intermittent company added to the enjoyment of their stay as he revisited his own tales from the past. His short-term memory and physical well-being may have suffered over the years, but his youthful twinkle would surface as he renewed moments from his early years.

On the fourth day of their 'holiday', Rosemary, Penny and Rosie sat with abandonment, laughing over further tales of guests and local characters, helping themselves to the olives they had picked themselves and other culinary delights. Rosie particularly enjoyed the golden olive liquid, poured generously on the fresh, crusty bread, mixed with the dark, thick balsamic vinegar. She relished the experience of trying new foods, the herbs and various green leaves, hiding scattered treasures of a creamy white cheese and succulent grapes or tomatoes; tastes that stimulated her senses, so different from the bland, salty or sweet tastes of her British palette.

"Let's go for a pizza tonight in the village," Rosemary advocated, enthused by her company's undeniable delight of the foods she had been serving.

It was quite a walk to the pizzeria, just outside the village. It was a converted space, at the side of a family home, which grew various herbs and vegetables. A large pen of chickens and a few sheep grazing on a field, part of their grounds, provided some of the ingredients for their small restaurant. There were five of them, Gina and Stanley joining the trio, so with some extravagance, Rosemary telephoned Enzo, the local gardener, builder and taxi driver, to carry the three of them there and back, followed by the truck, driven by Gina and accompanied by Stanley.

They arrived at the small brick building, perched neatly against the main building, set back off the road, hidden from the general public, but regarded warmly by the locals, as "the best place to eat in the whole of Italy". It was run by a loud, effusive Italian family, who spoke only Italian, and very fast, with the exception of their young son of about ten years old, who had picked up a few helpful English and French words and phrases at the local school and from the occasional foreign visitors. He was ambitious, even at such a young age. He had studied languages enthusiastically, convinced it would support the business, which would one day be his. The doors and windows were open, but nets were nailed across to keep out bugs and insects. Inside, out of the sun, it was shaded and dark, but cool and restful. Just outside, a display of a few eclectic tables under a wooden canopy, adorned with grapevines, creeping unrestrainedly over the frame, added a further extension. The visitors chose the latter, knowing they would soon be leaving for England, back to the unpredictable British weather.

Their large-bosomed host arrived, with a candle, not for its romantic connotations, but to alleviate the pests. More bread, olive oil and balsamic vinegar adorned the tables, placed in small wicker baskets, tempting their appetites, accompanied with sun-dried tomatoes and more olives. Rosie was going to miss such foreign delights and vowed to take some bottles home with her.

The pizzas arrived. The cream crust, browned convincingly along the edges, crunched and crumbled as they cut into the bread. The white, creamy cheese caught on the fork, leaving a trail of sticky thread. Rosie's attention was caught by the Italian family behind her, jabbering in Italian, happy, laughing and eating, relaxed, enjoying the pleasures of the dishes that ordained their table. She realised how much she was missing her own family. The bewitching sun setting slowly, hidden for a moment behind a few trees, was a distraction from her thoughts, and just then she felt very lucky.

The journey back to the villa was generally quiet, punctuated with talk of the wonderful meal and wine, the people and the views. The car was parked at the top of the hill, as it was easier for Enzo to turn around. They climbed out of his little Fiat and made their way back to the house. Stanley and Gina were waiting by the door, sitting on the wall, engaged in easy talk. Stanley had seemed more alive since the arrival of these guests, Rosemary had thought, but now he looked tired. Rosie gave him a helping hand as they walked over the stones and step, into the hallway and to the sitting room, where they would settle for half an hour or so, before retiring to bed.

It was Thursday morning. The sun, the insistent chirruping of the birds, the pungent, rich flowers and rich greens wrapped them and protected them from any troubles that might be haunting them. They would be flying home tomorrow and planned to enjoy the relaxing, sleepy hours on sunbeds around the pool, eating and drinking the tastes of Italy, sporadically pursuing the delights of the local area, and allowing their problems to melt into the distance on this, their last day. As the tired, satisfied guests indulged in Tuscany's delight into the late afternoon, Rosie suddenly cried out:

"Sam!"

They were not flying back until late afternoon the following day and, despite their attempts to contact Marjorie and Jim, there was no way of knowing what had disturbed Rosie so violently this second time. She had always worried about her brother, but this was different. Her mind had been awash with thoughts of Italy. She had not 'seen' anything, although she had been absorbed with thoughts of ten years ago and this she knew would affect any other concerns. She had welcomed the pleasures of the past few days, but now such distractions had come to a sudden and dramatic halt. Everyone was worried now and the end of the holiday had been brought forward abruptly and unkindly. They sat trying to enjoy the barbeque that evening but were preoccupied with thoughts of home. They endeavoured to regain the idle chat and calm which they had enjoyed, making the most of their last day, but the underlying worry nagged incessantly. Gina contacted the station, but there were no reports of any incidents that might involve her brother. It was after eleven o'clock the following morning: she received the telephone call while they were packing their bags into Rosemary's truck and a neighbour's car, to take them back to the airport. She decided to keep the news to herself. There was nothing anyone could do now. It would wait until they returned home.

CHAPTER 12

No one saw it coming. It was Paul who found him.

"I like her," Sam had commented on the latest pretty girl he was talking to. She was only about fifteen, he was thinking. She was sitting with an older friend at the bar.

"Yes. She's pretty enough. A bit young, though, to waste too much time and money on. Now, the older one, she might be worth a try." Sam thought Paul's attitude to women might be due to his own issues with his mother and tried to ignore his sexist comments. Paul grinned at his friend and laughed. He was just having a laugh with him. Sam was barely much older than the girl and he teased him about fancying her. Sam had been so upbeat when he arrived; he was helping Paul's mother around the house, cheerful and keen to enjoy his time in London. Paul was working behind a bar part-time, four nights including a Friday and Saturday, in a local club. He was enjoying it. He had charmed a few girls into bed, but nothing serious. Sam hooked up with Paul's mate Terry, when he was at work on the Saturday. They made their way round a few pubs, ending the night at the club where Paul worked, amusing themselves with a couple of early morning drinks, before going home.

The club closed at one o'clock and Paul finished up and joined them about half past one. He was tired but buzzing as he greeted his two friends, staggering about outside. There was a light drizzle, but no one seemed to notice. They followed Paul down the path towards the car park babbling on about where they had been and an incident with 'a couple of birds', and Paul told them about a pretty, dark-haired girl who hadn't left the bar most of the night. She had obviously fancied him, but he had been too busy to stop and chat. He had written his phone number on her hand.

The three of them jumped into his Aunt Julie's car. Paul only ever had one or two drinks at work; he was too busy to drink them anyway. It was kind of her to lend him the car when she was not using it for work. He knew of a few people who would drive after four or five pints, but he could not afford to chance it and lose his licence. The police hung around town after eleven o'clock, looking to stop any youths who might be drinking and driving. There had been a lot about dangerous driving in the papers, blaming young, careless and drunk drivers for most of the fatalities. Terry and Sam, quite drunk, were giggling like schoolkids over some stupid jokes. There would be no sense from them tonight! Paul thought. He dropped Terry off at the top of the road and watched him stumble towards his house. It was a rough area. He did not want to hang around long, but he waited long enough to see his mate arriving safely at his front door. Paper blew tirelessly round a drain, splattered with cigarette butts of a dubious kind. Grime and rubble surrounded the weeds of the broken paths. Greying curtains hung listlessly at the windows, the shabbiness of the dwellings punctuated occasionally by a tidy home, painted with care, fronted by a neat lawn and shrubs. A sign of hope.

Paul parked the car. Sam was sobering up. He had nodded off a couple of times in the short time it took for them to get home.

"Terry's mad, but I like him," Sam laughed.

"Yes, well, just don't get involved in any of his scams and dealings. His family are a bunch of crooks." He felt protective all of a sudden for his younger half-brother and gave him a friendly nudge.

"Come on, you – you're pissed!" There were still two beds in his room, the one that was his mother's, which he now used, and the smaller Z bed that was his and now used on occasion for his mates if they stayed over. Most of the time it was used as a couch for him to lounge on while he watched the portable television that Terry had got for him cheap. He had promised to look out for a new stereo, but Terry's bargains were dubious, and he had declined the offer. Sam was arranged awkwardly now across the small bed. Paul was enjoying his company and smiled with some contentment as he leant over to switch off the light.

They both slept late that morning; Paul to catch up the lack of sleep from working so late, Sam to rid himself of the hangover he was nursing. They mooched around the house, helping themselves to cereals and toast, reminiscing over a cup of tea. They talked about Sam's grandparents, of Sylvia mostly, and Paul talked sporadically about his aunt and his mum, the times he remembered before Gavin; memories of his childhood that best depicted her as a carefree young woman, beautiful and loving her little boy, although much of what he could remember related to the couple of Polaroid snaps fading in his drawer. He encouraged Sam to delve into his childhood memories; he wanted to know as much as possible about this family he had suddenly found himself connected to, by fate.

When his aunt returned from work late that afternoon, they sat around the small kitchen table, eating fish finger sandwiches in a casual family group that reminded Sam of another image of his past.

"Shall we walk down to the local?" Julie suggested to the two young men occupying her sofa. Paul was keen to go out and socialise: he needed some fresh air and the house seemed rather cramped with the three of them there.

"You two go, I'll stay here. I need to phone home and I'm off tomorrow afternoon. I need to pack. Anyway, I don't suppose you two get much time together, working shifts all the time," he added thoughtfully. They did not get much time together these days; they were both busy, and this week, while he had his friend to stay, they had hardly spoken or seen each other. So, they left Sam settled in front of the television and went out.

It was just after 10.30 when they got back. The house seemed uncannily quiet. Assuming Sam had gone to bed, Julie said, "Goodnight," and went off to her own bedroom. Paul opened the door noiselessly, so as not to disturb him. The first thing he saw was his white trainers, hanging limply in mid-air. Sam was hanging from a cord tugging into the flesh of his neck, tied tightly to the wire flex of the light in the centre of the room. A chair lay abandoned clumsily, on the carpet.

"No! No! No!" Paul grabbed the chair, climbing onto it and resting the loose feet onto it, to allow some slack.

"Help! Julie...Mum!" He wrestled frantically with the cord as it clung mercilessly to the heavy weight. His cries brought Julie rushing from her room. She stopped motionless in the doorway and then sprang into action. She rang for an ambulance and grabbed a knife from the kitchen drawer. She handed it to Paul, giving orders to the shocked and stunned young man who was wild and crazy in grief.

"Mum," he sobbed again, this time the word sinking deep into Julie's heart, squeezing it as tight as the cord around the boy's neck, "he's my brother, he's my brother." With a jolt the body fell back into his arms and he lay cradling it as he wept. Julie felt his grief. He had been like a brother to Paul. She moved behind him, tenderly supporting her 'son' in her arms, rocking him like a baby as he held the motionless body. Julie knew there was nothing anyone could do for him now. Paul continued to sob, like a wild wolf for its dead cub. She was alarmed by such unabashed grief but presumed he had been holding onto grief for so long, holding his feelings in a fist-like grip for so many years, that now he had abandoned himself to his pent-up feelings.

As he was carried out of the house, covered by a blanket, Julie went back inside to make a phone call she knew would cause unbearable pain to his family. The phone rang for a few minutes, the ringtone's constant, rhythmic shrill unnerving her more and more, until she heard a soft voice at the end of the line whispering in the dark. She suddenly realised it must be quite late. They were probably in bed asleep.

"Hello. Who is this?"

"It's Julie, Paul's aunt. There's been an accident. It's Sam." She found the words clicking like rehearsed lines in a play. "He's gone. He's gone." She knew she could not say any more.

"Gone? Gone where?" Her heart was aching, for him and for the family she hardly knew. But she continued with some simple facts, to stabilise her emotions.

"He's at Saint Jude's Hospital. You need to come right away. I'm so sorry." He fumbled for a pen or a pencil in the telephone table and wrote the address on the front of the telephone directory, in a controlled daze. He said, "Thank you," and blindly put down the phone, climbing the stairs in a trance as he worked his was up towards the bedroom, where his wife would be waiting for news she did not want to hear.

The slow walk along the corridor seemed endless.

"You always worried about your brother, Rosie, and I told you not to."

Her mother hugged her solid and deep.

"I couldn't help him. I couldn't help any of them." Rosie was thinking now of her grandfather, grandmother, of Sam and of Lucy. So much death, so much loss. She sat heavily on the chair next to Paul and held his hand, enduring their heartache together. His aunt was at home, waiting for his return.

"I need to get home." Jim did not hear him; consumed with his own misery but Marjorie had watched the way these two young people clung to each other for support and suddenly wanted to get away, away from the hospital, from Jim and from anything that reminded her of the dead body of her precious son.

"I will go. I'll go and check on your aunt. You stay here with Rosie and I'll meet you all back home. I need to get out of here." No one had the energy to argue or the willpower to change the plan. She walked with a desperate energy, until she reached the glass doors and the cold rush of air as she pushed one open. It was as heavy as her heart. She didn't hear Jim call after her. She didn't hear anything as she was driven by a blind panic towards the car park outside. As she glanced up, her eyes blurred with the tears, she noticed a phone box. She scrabbled around in her handbag and then her pockets for tenpence. She needed to talk to Penny. Just as she felt the hard, round metal coin in her hand, she felt the weight of an arm and allowed herself to be engulfed in the solid arms of her husband.

"Oh Jim!" They were absorbed in their own shared wretchedness, when Penny and John arrived.

It was a long night. Penny offered to take Marjorie round to see Paul's aunt. John had booked rooms in a hotel nearby. He drove Jim and Rosie there, taking Paul, too. He and Rosie seemed to be supporting each other. Jim still in shock, consumed in his own silence. When Penny arrived at Julie's house, she dropped Marjorie off and went back to the hotel as she requested.

"Just ring me at the hotel and I will come and pick you up."

Julie recognised the woman on her doorstep and was surprised by her appearance.

"Paul wanted to stay. He and Rosie seem to need each other at the moment," she explained.

"I didn't realise how much Sam meant to him. He thought of him as a brother."

"Well, he was, well, half-brother anyway."

Julie's eyes were searching. "What do you mean?"

It wasn't until that moment that Marjorie was aware that

this woman had no idea of her sister's relationship with her husband. She was not quite sure what to say.

"Have you talked to Paul about his relationship with Sam?"

"Relationship? They were very close friends. They weren't…"

She paused awkwardly. Marjorie was not quite sure what she was implying. Despite the consequences, she did not think the situation could get much worse. She took another sip of the tea, now lukewarm and began to tell her story, skipping a few details that were too hard to speak aloud. As she watched Julie's face harden and pale, Marjorie was unexpectedly distracted by the cup she was holding in her hand. She had not noticed it before, caught up in their conversation. It had a pale blue background, with delicate pink flowers, the rim touched with a delicate, golden edge.

"I need you to go." She was tight-lipped and struggling with this woman's presence. This woman's husband had made her sister pregnant, he had abandoned her and now she was dead. She was not sure whether it was shock or anger she felt from these revelations, but she was hurt that Paul had kept this all from her.

"I'm sorry," was all Marjorie could think of saying. She got up to leave. She felt ashamed and guilty and angry with Jim. Angry with everyone now, crumbling again with the loss of her son, she staggered out of the front door then sat on Julie's doorstep and wept. The door opened gingerly.

"Come inside." Julie bent down and helped Marjorie up, ushering her back into the living room.

"He knew you would be angry. That's why Paul didn't tell you. He sees you as his mum, but he and his father, Jim, are getting on well. He likes being part of the family." Marjorie was trying to clarify everything for her, but it all sounded awkward. She wasn't even sure how she was feeling right then. They both sat quietly. Julie rested her hand on Marjorie's arm. Suddenly she was drawn by the tea set again.

"Where did you get the tea set? It's exactly the same as my mother-in-law's. It's such a beautiful pattern. I always loved it."

"Paul gave it to me for my birthday, a long time ago. His friend had a brother who bought and sold antiques. It is beautiful, isn't it? I don't get it out very often." The women were absorbed for a moment, preoccupied with their own memories and the delightful, delicate china. I have a couple of other pieces. She pointed to a vase tucked away in the corner on a shelf. Marjorie let out a small gasp. It was Sylvia's, she was sure.

"Jim's mum had one just like it, but her window cleaner had befriended her and taken it, as well as a tea set just like this one," she explained tentatively.

"What did he look like?" Julie suddenly alert to her words.

"Well, my mother-in-law described him to Sam as rather rugged-looking but with sexy eyes." Mentioning his name, suddenly brought fresh tears cascading down her face. She found Julie easy to talk to and opening up like this was both a relief and unnerving. She was conscious now that her words had been accusatory and she was embarrassed.

"It could have been Terry's brother, Nick. Oh Marjorie. I am sorry. I think they may have been hers. I was never convinced by how Paul had acquired them, but he was so excited about giving me them. I didn't like to press him too much about where he bought them or who from." The conversation had changed entirely and somehow connected them to the past. There was a brief, stunned silence, before Marjorie suggested she rang Penny for a lift back to the hotel.

"Let me drive you," she offered.

"Thank you." As Marjorie climbed into the car, she turned to Julie.

"Let's not worry about the china just now."

CHAPTER 13

Gina had not personally had dealings with Nick Jackson, but she knew of him. He had been arrested for handling stolen goods years ago when he was still a teenager. He had been arrested again for theft and grievous bodily harm and was now in prison on a drugs charge; he was due out in two years. There was no evidence to link him to the burglary at Sylvia Birch's home all those years ago, but the stolen items seemed to match those found in Julie's apartment and Paul had admitted to buying them from his brother. He did not want to get Terry into trouble, though, and now that the Birches had their valuables back, they did not want to press charges. There was too much grief at the moment; they did not want to cause further heartache. Terry had enough problems surviving with a family like that. But Gina had another interest in this Nick Jackson. She wanted to ask him about a drug he might have sold to a pretty, blonde woman a decade ago.

She was led through the secured gates into a waiting area. The room was stuffy. Several tables were laid out regimentally in rows, a chair on either side. A diverse group of visitors were talking to loved ones. A large man, with tattoos engraved on his hefty, hairy arms, sat fiddling with his sleeve as he waited for someone to arrive. She recognised the inmate she had come to see immediately. His hair was lank, but his eyes were still attractive. Nick watched her walk towards him and sit down. He fixed his gaze on this dark-haired woman, smiling with an appreciative satisfaction and charm. He was happy to admit and tell all. It would not affect his parole. He had done his time. He was only helping the young woman in a difficult situation. He remembered Lucy. He had tried to come on to her. She was older, but very attractive and she had spirit. She could do a lot better than that boyfriend of hers, although no one could argue he had a lot of money! Yes, he had given her the drug.

"I'll track him down for you. I could have him wasted… when I get out," he boasted.

"Well, I would appreciate the offer of finding him, but I think you should let the police handle the rest, don't you?" Nick grinned wolfishly. "Whatever…"

"I expect we will meet again, but I hope not. Thank you for your honesty and help." She was feeling generous towards him. He had helped a lot and she could not help but be a little dazzled by his charms.

Back in the office she wrote up her report. The funeral was tomorrow and Ian had given her a couple of hours off to attend. She was back on course for promotion now. Her hard work was paying off and the friendship she had established with Rosie she knew would help her in the future, even though neither of them admitted it aloud.

"I'm changing my course next year from a BA in Law to a degree in Criminal Law and Forensics. It's a bit specialised but it's what I'm interested in," she had told Gina, a couple of weeks ago. She had waited for a sign of approval from this woman who had become her friend and mentor.

"Well, I think it's a good idea. And you might see more in the clues than anyone else on the course."

Rosie smiled lightly and then they were caught in generous laughter, feeling the relief this burst of joviality brought at such a difficult time.

Rosie went with her mother to the airport. Marjorie was very nervous after all this time. She was excited, too. A welcome relief to the desperate anguish that had swallowed her up. They had forged a deep love all those years ago. Their yearly Christmas letters were lengthy, summarising the year's events with additional photographic evidence that had ordained the mantelpiece as a reminder of the family so far away. Although it had taken the death of her son to bring them together again, the long-awaited reunion of the sisters had come at last.

Waiting eagerly at the Arrivals gate, Marjorie and Rosie watched the people filtering through the glass doors. Despite knowing from the various photographs sent over the years that Eileen's son Will looked a lot like Sam, Rosie heard the sharp intake of her mother's breath as soon as they saw him. It was uncanny and rather unnerving. He had Sam's blue-green eyes. His hair was parted to the side just like Sam's, and he bustled forward with a similar excitable energy. The tall, dark girl beside him was probably about eight or nine years old and, although she looked quite plain, when she smiled there was an obvious likeness to her aunt. The sisters embraced with a deep longing and the children smiled congenially at each other.

The church was packed for the funeral. Gina stood at the back watching and feeling the grief of this family. They had already been through so much. They still had not been able to trace Gavin Jameson, but she would not give up. The police were satisfied that Jim Birch was a victim rather than a suspect now, and, although the case remained open, he had not been charged and the case had been filed away, for now. Jim and Marjorie stood shakily, clutching each other to keep the strength that was waning as the vicar spoke. Rosie and Paul stood side-by-side at the front, giving their short eulogies to the sea of tearful faces. Paul's aunt sat quietly next to them, with a friend from work. The Australian family were seated behind and, although most eyes were on Sam's parents and their daughter, Rosie was conscious of the impact William had had on the congregation. The small boy fidgeted, embarrassed by this attention. Rosie saw Will's sister Jenny squeeze his hand reassuringly. She was suddenly reminded of the time she had held her little brother's hand as they walked to school together and her heart ached. It ached further when she realised her mother was watching them, too, and had recognised the gesture, too, linking it to her memory when she held her little sister's hand tightly at the farm, as the large, scruffy chicken, with scruffy feathers, waddled up to them suspiciously, followed by others and Eileen began to cry.

For Paul's mum Julie, the whole situation seemed like a weird dream that she could not make sense of, but her place was with Paul and she had counselled Marjorie on a few occasions. She liked her, although she avoided Jim. She hoped she could overcome the anger she felt towards him one day. At the moment, the hostility she felt towards him still simmered but the anger and hate were now directed clearly at Gavin Jameson. If that was his real name. Penny stood behind Marjorie with her sister and a few of their friends, her hand gently resting on her shoulder briefly, in recognition of her heartbreak. And John held his supportive arm around Penny's waist.

Others sat and stood through the service, all wondering why such a young man should have brought them all here today in shared grief. Patrick and Brenda Blakey, their daughter Susan and son-in-law Richard bowed their heads in prayer. Brenda was thinking fondly of the little boy who had been so full of life, playing in the back garden, all those years ago. Susan watched Rosie, so grown up now, still with those dark, penetrating eyes, now full of heavy tears for her brother. She wanted to hug her and tell her everything would be alright, comfort her the way she had been comforted when they were just children. Now, she hardly knew her. "I will get to know her again," she promised herself as she leant quietly on the arm of her husband.

As Rosie followed her parents down the aisle, towards the hefty oak doors, she looked randomly about her, at the faces watching them and sharing their sorrow. She did not recognise many, her eyes blurred with tears, and her mind was restless, trying to contain her pain. She noticed Mrs Lyons, though, from their primary school. She looked very old now. She was so kind to Sam. She believed in him, unlike some of the other teachers who would send him out or hit his knuckles with the ruler for talking. She smiled at her and knew that it meant a lot to the aging woman who had given her life and energy to teaching so many small children, watching them grow, move on and hoping they would have good, successful lives. Sam's death was her loss, too. The man beside her she recognised as Mac, from her father's work. He had always supported her dad, even when he nearly lost his job. The company wanted to sack him when he was arrested but he managed to persuade them to give him extended leave until 'it was all sorted out', convincing them it was all a mistake. Now he, too, looked crumpled at the weight of such a waste of life.

Geoff and his new girlfriend, Sophie, stood at the back a fair distance from Penny and John. A quick glance from Geoff towards Penny revealed their guilty past for an instant, but they had all moved on. Geoff was here because he felt the need to support John and the Birches in their terrible grief. He had really liked Sam, who had worked for him at times doing some manual work for a bit of pocket money. Like everyone else there that day, he was thinking, "How could such a lively young man, with everything to live for, do such a thing? His poor parents and sister."

As Rosie passed, Gina connected with her momentarily with a consolatory nod and joined the last few people outside. Just the immediate family went back to the house: Marjorie, Jim, Penny, John, Rosie and Paul. Rosie reached out naturally and held Paul's hand again, as they stood in the hallway alone, before assembling in the kitchen for a few nibbles and therapeutic alcohol.

"I'm going to have a son and call him Sam," Rosie pronounced. Paul was not sure whether she was making a decision or predicting what she already knew. Her gift may have saved her father and helped bring the family together, but she hadn't been able to save Sam and that would plague her for the rest of her life. Rosie at that moment felt her gift wasn't a gift at all, but she also knew, because her grandmother had told her, that she was special. She needed to look after her gift – it was unpredictable – and

as she let go of Paul's hand and turned to look out of the
window, she was aware of a young man crossing the street.
"Simon, that's Simon," she told herself. And she knew that
he was going to be important in her life as she watched him
disappear around the corner.

ABOUT THE AUTHOR:

A retired English teacher, born in Essex in 1960, she has been writing stories and poetry since childhood and recently self-published her first collection of poems: Life's Journey Through Poetry.

Rosie's Gift is her first novel. Collating various pieces of inspired writing and plot ideas, this is a culmination of personal memories, integrated into a fictional crime story. Since retiring from teaching; writing, painting and babysitting her granddaughter Mae, have become her full-time career.